Walker

Authored by: Jennifer McGee

Laura's Story

"Every man has his secret sorrows which the world knows not; and often times we call a man cold when he is only sad." – Henry Wadsworth Longfellow

Prologue:

I remember being exhausted when I asked my grandmother to come and stay with me for a few days. I was a middle school principal, I had two toddlers, and I had a husband who held the prehistoric belief system that his work was outside, and mine was inside. That meant he got to snow blow the driveway for the occasional blizzard or mow the lawn weekly, but in the meantime, the daily dishes, the cooking, the laundry, and the cleaning all belonged to me. It was bullshit, but it was what I married.

I was overwhelmed, and my children had all of the childhood illnesses that go along with wintertime in Maine. They had croup. They had ear infections. They had constant runny noses. I had used up my fair share of family sick days, and had missed enough work staying at home with my hacking, coughing, feverish toddlers, that I was running behind at school and feeling bad Mommy guilt and simultaneous school principal guilt.

My husband was out of town on business, so I took a chance and called my grandmother to see if she could come and help with the children. To my great relief, she agreed and arrived at my doorstep the next day with an overnight tote bag in one hand and a pan of those remarkable chocolate, butterscotch laden, coco-nutty homemade gooey magic bars topped with foil in the other. I instantly blinked back tears, grateful at the sight of my very own Mary Poppins.

When I got home from school on the first night of Gram's visit, it was already dark and I was completely out of gas. The children ran to greet me at the door, blessedly, fresh out of the bathtub. Their hair was still wet and they smelled of baby powder and Vicks Vapo-rub. An aromatic vat of chicken stew with doughy, plump dumplings bubbled on the back burner of the stove, and the clusterfuck of our living room landmine of toddler toys had been neatly sorted and shelved.

The four of us, my grandmother, my two children, and I sat together around the kitchen table, which was set with placemats, long forgotten cloth napkins and another rare sight, full sets of silverware, and together, we had dinner. Before we ate, Grammy asked to say a blessing. I quickly pretended this was a ritual my children were familiar with, although they immediately blew my cover when they looked confused as she asked us to bow our heads. As Gram thanked the Lord for the "food we were about to receive" I was instantly grateful for the moment we were sharing. For a blessed moment in time, I got to jump off the hamster wheel and was reminded of simpler times.

That night, after we tucked in the children, each with their own choice of a bedtime story, I poured a glass of wine and offered one to Grammy. She balked for a second, and then said, "Oh heck. Why not?" with a little twinkle in her eye. As I handed a chilled goblet of sauvignon blanc to her, we sat back in the living room, and I confessed something I hadn't told anyone.

Taking a deep breath, I told her my dirty little secret. "Gram, I'm not happy in my marriage." It was all I said, but it was big for me, as I hadn't ever said those words out loud before. The statement just sat there for a moment like a helium balloon losing its air in the center of the room, awkwardly hanging.

Gram leaned forward, and looked directly at me. "Well," she said frankly and unflinchingly, "whoever told you you had to be happy?"

Her words took me aback. I wasn't sure what I thought I would hear, but in looking back at that moment, I am certain that was not the response I had been hoping for. I think I just quietly took another sip of wine, experiencing an unfamiliar loss for words.

As the night wore on, Gram, for the first time, told me her story.

It was interesting. Until that evening, our relationship had been so egocentric. She had simply been "**my** grandmother." Her role in my life had always been the fawning, adoring, old woman who knit me sweaters, sewed me tiny Barbie outfits, and made me her favorite lunch, fried bologna sandwiches. She and I spent hours making up new hilarious and silly verses to the poem "Higgilty Piggilty My Fat Hen."

That night, for the first time, however, my perspective changed entirely. It was the first time I saw her through a new lens. She was a woman, just like me. She was, in fact, part of the sisterhood. One of millions of females trying to do the best we can with the life we find ourselves leading.

And all women share the complexities of figuring out their place in the world...we are daughters, we are sisters, we are wives, we are mothers, we are grandmothers. Sometimes, we just are...

This is the story of my grandmother. Laura was her name.

Chapter 1:

The tension rose from her chest constricting her breathing. Her nerves had become a rope, tightening their coiled fibers around her neck. She lurched forward, gasping, dropping Norman's spoon into the metal sink with a percussive clang as she made her way through the kitchen.

She grabbed desperately at her red gingham apron, pulling its ties urgently away from her neck, and tugging it away from her waist. It was choking her. She couldn't breathe. She lunged at the screen door, dropped the apron to the ground, shoving the door open in desperation for the air to fill her lungs. She ran down the weather beaten front steps, bending at the waist, heart pounding, swallowing giant gulps of blessed fresh air that tasted of earth.

Running her hands through masses of unruly mahogany curls, forehead damp with sweat, she slowly stood and steadied her breathing. Calm down now, Laura, for the love of God was the mantra, repeating, inside of her head. Calm down. Calm down. Calm down.

Looking out from tamped down grasses that formed the walkway of her childhood home, out at the view from Walker Hill, she was reminded that the world was not so small.   Just her world was small. Her world was microscopic in dimensions,

suffocating and narrow.

The field grasses caught her attention. When the wind blew just right, it was as if all of

the grasses were dancing. First all the long blades would sway to the right, emerald

greens, tans and browns, and pale greens and forest greens. The fronds would stand

straight up, pause, and then bow to the front, and then dip, over and over. The

symphonic whoosh and whirs of the blades were mesmerizing. Strands of her hair

blew from behind her ear, tangling tendrils around her face. Walker Hill.   For a place

in time, her whole life existed on this one unforgiving slope of landscape.

Could a place be both heaven and hell?

Red breasted robins, cedar waxwings, tiny chickadees, sparrows and wrens, giant

black crows, red winged blackbirds, and the occasional whirring humming birds.

Dipping up and down, in and out of the grasses. Chirps and warbles, tweets and caws.

The melodic sounds of childhood. In and out, up and down, they bobbed through the

grasses. The frenetic, cheerful, particular movement of the birds stood boldly in stark

contrast with the anguish and monotony being lived out just beyond, inside of the

house, on the knoll.

In the background, always in the full bloom of spring, the shrill constant trill of the

crickets. The buzzing vibration of giant lazy bumblebees…fat and drunk on the nectar of wildflowers lumbering along, visiting blossom after blossom….the white bloom of lilies of the valley, the proud yellow faces of daisies, the pink and white purple spikes of lupine dotting the horizon, the delicate and intricate lacy patterns of Queen Anne's lace. There was never a shortage of sweet nectar sips on Walker Hill.

Ma and Pa's listing and leaning barn seemed to balance on top of the swell of the hill. Crookedy wooden steps led to a smile of a front porch. Ma and Pa had hand-caned rocking chairs positioned with a wooden barrel between them, upside down for a table, to snip beans or shell peas in a bowl between. The front door held the only coat of paint on the house. Yellow…once cheerful and bright, now a, pale hue reminding all who entered of the optimism of yesteryears, like a dimming light.

Outside the clothesline almost always held sheets or towels or billowing shirts, flapping about wildly, fighting the wooden pegs which fastened them to the line against their will.

Winded and worn out after walking the steep path to the house, the barn boards of home reached out to the weary traveler, a welcome sight, no matter how tattered the shutters, regardless how chipped the paint. The path to the yellow door was a warm embrace.

Squinting out to the horizon, the tones of the earth soothed her, calmed her. Slowed her breathing. Somewhere in the distance, in the fields of lupine, she knew Pa stood, looking out at the great beyond, his eyes seeking answers in the distance. Pa said

Henry Wadsworth Longfellow was a distant relative. He took great pride in that fact,

and he often recited the words of his kin effortlessly into the abyss, arms flailing,

audience only in his mind:

> *Tell me not, in mournful numbers,*
>
> *Life is but an empty dream!*
>
> *For the soul is dead that slumbers,*
>
> *And things are not what they seem.*

His voice steady and strong trailing over and through the dancing weeds and blossoms.

She inhaled, deeply at the waist, one more time before turning toward the house.

Inside, she could hear the deep wracking coughs pulling her toward the yellow

door...while simultaneously pushing her away from the yellow door. Go in. Go in. Tend

them.

Ma's voice broke through the sounds of the cough, "Laura. Laura. Where the devil are

you?" Laura sighed and picked up the apron she had thrown to the ground. She pulled

the gingham ties to the back of her neck and formed a bow. She could feel the familiar

tightening around her throat as she thrust open the screen door.

Chapter 2:

Norman was Laura's first born. In 1938, only the well –to- do went to the hospital to give birth to their babies. Local midwives came to the bedside of the pregnant mothers with lesser means. Water was boiled. Foreheads were tamped. Just as movies depicted, rags were, in fact, prepared and made ready to absorb the fluids which would erupt during delivery.

Flora was the most commonly used midwife in Livermore Falls. Perhaps she was the only one. Sturdy and no nonsense, she had the reputation of an army sergeant. All of the local mothers in town, continued the lore of Flora. "She suffers no fools. When she tells you not to push you daren't exhale a breath." "I was so terrified of pushing that baby out against Flora's orders," one new mother exaggerated, "I held my breath for seven minutes."

Every bouncing, rosy- cheeked baby in town was Flora's claim to fame. When she sat at the Rexall counter having her root beer float, she would name every baby passing by the store window in a pram, telling the disinterested soda jerk the story of each birth. As she enthusiastically dipped the long handle of her spoon into the frothy dessert to dish out the vanilla ice cream, she would point out of the window, "Oh that's little Andrew. He was a stubborn sort, took me all night of my husband's 60th birthday…"

Nothing shocked or embarrassed Flora. She got a big, burly laugh out of the modest ladies as they tucked their nightclothes under their bums as their labor began. "Oh, that night gown will be wrapped around your neck by the time we're done here missy," she would say to the blushing young women, and sure enough, they would be on all fours by the end, pushing that baby through their never before exposed under parts, into the chapped and rugged, sure and steady hands of Flora Bean.

Flora was a lifelong, front pew member of the United Methodist Church congregation. Her spot in church was so secure that her name was written in the hymnal to ensure no newcomer would make the mistake of taking her seat. Reverend Henry Brooks was the quiet, handsome young minister of the church. He and his beautiful wife, Laura, had just recently moved into the church parsonage where all of the ministers and their families, before him, had lived.

On the first day of his ministry, as Henry Brooks was preaching, Flora sat bolt upright in the first pew, the same place she had been sitting since she was old enough to remember. As she cast her eyes sideways to have a look at the minister's wife, her trained eye immediately noticed the tiny bump in the midriff of, an otherwise very slender, Mrs. Brooks' cotton dress. She knew, out of the whole congregation, she would be the one to get to know the new minister's wife the best. She smiled knowingly as she opened her hymnal to *"Bringing in the Sheaves,"* and she raised her voice in tune with the choir, thoroughly enjoying this tasty little morsel of a most delicious secret.

Chapter 3:

"Talk not of wasted affection – affection never was wasted."

After the service, the Ladies' of the Methodist Church always provided a light luncheon. Since this was Reverend Brooks' first service, Flora could see they put some extra time and effort into their offerings. The women had an assortment of their own bone china plates, they had all brought from home, filled with sweet onion and ham sandwiches, fresh egg salad rolls, and dainty triangular sandwiches with creamed cheese and thinly sliced cucumbers. There were cut glass bowls brimming with sweet gherkin pickles and colorful fruit salad. For dessert, platters overflowed with lovely delicate, crisp thumbprint snicker doodles, and perfectly round sugar cookies sprinkled with confectionary sugar. At the very end of the buffet line, the proud and smiling white haired ladies spooned out ladles full of pulpy fruit punch with floating islands of ice cream sherbert. "Well done, I should say, well done," Flora winked at the women as she received her cup full of punch.

After walking away from the tables of food, balancing plate and cup, Flora made her way to Mrs. Brooks at the end of the fellowship hall. Although modestly dressed in a pale yellow shift with a brown cameo broach at the neckline, the midwife could see she was a rare and stunning natural beauty. She had high cheekbones, and huge brown eyes veiled in lashes that needed no mascara. Her lips were lightly tinged with a modest swipe of red lipstick. Mrs. Brooks immediately shifted her glance toward the fast- approaching Flora, and flashed a brilliant easy smile and an outstretched, gloved hand.

Flora was caught off guard by this forward and confident greeting, and quickly attempted to balance her plate more sturdily in her thick left hand. She then awkwardly attempted to shift her cup to the same hand, but blushed as she realized she was likely to dump the whole kit and caboodle! Mrs. Brooks realized that a handshake was not going to work in this circumstance and laughed airily, and instead patted Flora on the arm gently.

Flora realized she was off the hook and regained her composure. "Hello ma'am, welcome to Livermore," she said looking into Mrs. Brooks' eyes. "My name is Flora," and then, with a complete lack of subtlety glanced down to Mrs. Brooks' bulging midriff. "I am the local midwife in this town," she announced, with a firm concentration and emphasis on the word *midwife*, and then once again cast her eyes knowingly straight toward Mrs. Brooks. She could detect a slight blush rising into Mrs. Brooks' lovely cheekbones.

"My name is Laura," responded the young minister's wife with another dazzling smile, "and I think you and I will get to know each other very soon," acknowledging Flora's suspicions, and sweetly patting her swollen stomach.

Flora was given confidence then to talk extensively to Laura about her practice. She pointed around the fellowship hall to tow-headed little boys, and plaited little girls, noting she had a hand in delivering each of them. Laura could see the pride Flora took in her role, and hearing of each little human's entry into the world, at the hand of Flora, made her glad to make this sturdy little woman's acquaintance.

Laura noticed her husband, slight of build, but dashingly dark and handsome in his new black robe draped in an orchid colored prayer shawl, snaking his way through the congregation toward her. She grabbed his hand and proudly introduced him to Flora Bean.

"Henry," she said beaming at Flora, "meet the lady who will bring our first child into the world." Flora could not have looked more delighted with herself.

Chapter 4:

"In character, in manner, in style, in all things, the supreme excellence is simplicity."

Every two weeks or so, Laura and Flora made a point of getting together. In the living room of the modestly furnished parsonage, they would sip tea out of the blue and white, Willow Ware teacups left from the previous minister and his wife, and the minister before that, and the one before that one.

Laura always greeted Flora in a hand stitched day dress, the bow loosened more and more in the waist on each subsequent visit. Flora told Laura all about the town and the people in the town. Who could possibly know more than the local midwife about all of the people's lives in the village? Laura listened attentively to each and every tale of the families in the church. Although Laura was never one to initiate gossip, she also was not one to turn down the deliciousness of it when offered, and she provided a rapt audience for Flora every time they got together.

Laura enjoyed sharing tales of her own with her new friend and midwife. Flora learned that Laura was from Wilton, a town nearly 25 miles away from Livermore. Laura described the farmhouse she grew up in and she portrayed a poor, but dignified, life on the top of the highest hill in Wilton, Walker Hill. Laura's stories captured Walker Hill in rich and loving detail. Her words painted a landscape filled with natural, breathtaking beauty, and her descriptions sketched a simple and stark livelihood in a warm farmhouse atop of this massive, steep hill. Her Ma and Pa sounded like wonderfully stoic and self-reliant folks who remained quietly and happily separate from a changing, more industrialized civilization.

Flora was fascinated to learn about Laura's parents who still resided on Walker Hill, with no running water…just a pump from a well. Laura fondly recounted lining up with her two sisters and her brother, brushing their teeth over the wooden trough where the hand pump poured freezing cold spring water from a spout. She described the privy behind the house, and how she would wake her sisters in the middle of the night, so she didn't have to tiptoe outside, terrified of awakening a skunk or porcupine on her path to tinkle. If she could not find a partner to join her, she would tinkle in a porcelain chamber pot kept beneath her downy featherbed mattress. The two women laughed together as she described the thunderous noise, even a little girl, peeing in a pot, would make in the still of the night.

It was no wonder Laura seemed so delighted to be "in town," and she was obviously so appreciative of the parsonage in which she lived. She had all of the modern conveniences… an electric range that heated up with the turn of a dial, a sink with running hot and cold water, and a toilet that flushed. Laura took exceptional care of her new home, and tended every inch and corner of it with loving care.

Flora found it refreshing to meet such an unspoiled and grateful young bride. Flora had served on the Methodist Board of Ministries for years, and she would field the long string of complaints new minister's wives would issue to the board. She grew weary of the long list of demands those wives would make as they moved into the parsonage behind the church. But Laura never complained. Not a single gripe.

If there happened to be a worn spot on the back of the aging Windsor chair in the parsonage living room, Flora would notice a lace doily had been artfully placed over the thread worn material. On their frequent visits, Flora would see the remnants of paint colors under Laura's nail beds, and she would notice freshly painted cupboards, and the next week, the furniture on the porch would boast a brand new coat of paint. Laura was always busy, lovingly brightening every corner of her home.

As it turned out, Henry was not only an inspirational minister, but he also was a wonderful artist. Flora noticed his artwork adorned the walls of the parsonage, and the landscape Laura described from their childhoods, was also to be found in the artwork hanging in each room.

Yes, Laura was a breath of fresh air, in every possible way. She was lovely in appearance. She was unspoiled. She was handy. She was warm and kind. When her husband preached each Sunday, she sat in the front pew, just to the right of where Flora sat, and she never took her eyes off from Henry, her husband.

She nodded as Henry spoke from the pulpit. She smiled if he told a joke. Every now and again, she would glance around nervously to see if the congregation was enjoying him as much as she was. She looked delighted when they were laughing at his humor, and satisfied, she too would relax and laugh along with them.

One particular Sunday, when she was all but bursting with her unborn baby, a fly kept darting and hovering all around Reverend Brooks' head. She must have been overtired. Flora knew all too well how hard it becomes to sleep when a baby is close to delivery. That fly struck Laura's funny-bone.

As Reverend Brooks swatted and batted the fly away while continuing to deliver his sermon, Laura got an uncharacteristic fit of the giggles. The fly swarmed and dove, and landed atop Henry's head, and Laura was nearly hysterical with silent, suppressed laughter, tears streaming down her face. At one point, Henry noticed his wife's uncommon demeanor and lack of composure, and he, too, began to laugh.

Well Flora could hardly believe it. The whole congregation got into the joke, and everyone was laughing.

This little couple, Reverend and Mrs. Brooks, brought something fresh and new and wonderful to Livermore Falls. New England churches are known for their somber services....their dark organ music....their scolding, dark messages to the congregation. A church full of laughter was almost unheard of. Now that was something brand new, and quite frankly, completely delightful!

As the parishioners filed out of the church, each family greeted Reverend and Mrs. Brooks before heading to the refreshments downstairs, as was the long-standing tradition. There was a particular, tangible warmth and an embrace of this couple that was decidedly different. Flora would never forget the Sunday service where the fly took over the sermon.

Chapter 5:

"Into each life, some rain must fall."

It was midnight. She had heard the distinctive cuckoo sounding from the clock downstairs as it called out twelve clear tones. The pains started gradually, as is often the way. Deep in the small of her back, Laura felt the urgent and undeniable calling of her boy. She first quietly snuck out of bed, in the dark, and tiptoed down the parsonage steps, trying not to wake Henry.

Once downstairs, she turned the knob of the lamp in the kitchen, and filled the teapot with water from the tap. She would attempt to relax by sipping some chamomile tea, and pace to see if walking would relieve the pressure and hurry the labor along. Perhaps this little one decided to make his appearance following all of the laughter in church.

Laura looked down at her churning huge belly. "So, little one. You love the sound of laughter do you?" and she steeped her tea in her blue Willow Ware cup. She purposely chose the cup with the blue windmills, as she was certain she was carrying a boy.

Ma told her she would crave salt if it were a boy and she would crave sweets if it was a girl, and she definitely yearned for crisp bacon, and found herself putting extra salt pork into her baked beans on Saturday nights.

She abandoned the notion of walking, as that sort of movement felt far too taxing, so instead she picked up her knitting from the basket next to her rocking chair. She quietly admired her own neat handiwork, as she placed the needle and soft gray yarn in her lap. She thought she might as well finish up his baby bunting for those chilly days and nights. She imagined placing him in his soft bunting, and then lowering him into his carriage. She would walk him to the Rexall downtown, and she would show him off to all who came to the counter. Without warning, a searing pain in her abdomen stopped her mid-reverie.

Between her legs, she was surprised and alarmed to feel the warm rush of fluid. And then, as she was still trying to evaluate all that was happening to her, a stabbing pain tore through her like a sword piercing through her middle. She dropped the knitting and lunged out of the chair, stumbling briefly into the stand holding her blue and white teacup. The sound of the glass breaking woke Henry and he ran down the stairs, calling her name, "Laura…"

Her terrified eyes met his. She looked down at the fluids pooled at her feet, the broken glass….her own wetness, and the puddle of her tea. Sweat beaded on her forehead, and she desperately reached for his hand, "Oh the pain, Henry. Oh, it hurts…" Her hand found his in the darkness of the night. His hand was ice cold. He was frightened too.

She tried to remember what Flora told her. She knew once the fluid sac broke, the baby was on his way, and as Flora said, "no ifs, ands or buts". She also knew it would hurt, but the enormous foreboding fear she felt. She didn't expect to feel so frightened. Terrified really. She was faint and her knees were weak with it.

"Let me get Flora," Henry said, pulling on a shoe, hopping on one foot. "I will bike to her house Lolly." Henry nicknamed Laura, Lolly, and always called her that in the privacy of their home. "I will be gone for just a flash. Are you good now Lolly? Can you hold on?" he said haltingly as he backed out the front door, and she knew she had no choice.

As her husband ran into the night, leaving Laura alone and frightened, she wished Ma was with her. She imagined Ma on Walker Hill. She wondered if her mother knew? If she was suddenly awakened in the night, connected spiritually with her daughter in need. It was nice to think that maybe Ma was awake, pacing the floor along with her.

Thinking about Ma soothed her. Ma had four babies on Walker Hill. She didn't have a mid-wife. She just had neighbors. She had been just fine. She gave birth to four healthy babies, and all had been born right up on the farm. It would be okay.

Flora would help her through this. She pictured Flora's sturdy, capable hands. She remembered Flora pointing out all of the healthy, pink-cheeked children in the parish. This one. That one. She had delivered them all. Yes, surely Flora would be Laura's saving grace tonight.

And then the pain grabbed her again. Deep, deep primal cramping, located in regions of her body she had never known existed until this very moment. She grabbed the back of the rocking chair, and gritted her teeth not even recognizing the sounds she was making as she fought the pain.

Please Henry, please get here. She closed her eyes picturing the fields of Walker Hill: the tall lupine, the lilies of the valley, the wild Indian paintbrushes. As she envisioned the sloping fields of her childhood, the primal pain which connected every mother on the face of the earth coursed through her body.

Ma, oh Ma, I need you Ma.

She heard the blessed sound of the parsonage screen door flying opening. A breathless Henry and Flora entered the kitchen. A red-faced, panting Flora carried her satchel in hand. Laura noted, that although winded, pure and radiant confidence was glowing on Flora's face.

Chapter 6:

"A feeling of sadness and longing, that is not akin to pain...."

Once settled in bed, sheets placed beneath her nether regions, Flora pulled a stool to the foot of the bed, and leaned in between Laura's thighs, as she had done hundreds of times with hundreds of women before this night.

Laura gripped the sheets, locking the fabric between her fingers as if she could rip it away with every swelling pain tearing through her abdomen. Moans erupted from the cavity of Laura's throat, the sounds shamed Laura yet she could not manage to suppress them. Flora placed her hands on Laura's kneecaps and shook her head, clucking, "Mrs. Brooks, I am afraid we have a long way to go yet. Prepare yourself for an entire night of this, and maybe even a bit more. That baby is no where near ready to come out." Laura was devastated with that news, and cried out mournfully as another wave of pain gripped her.

The night wore on much the same. Laura, in moments of subsiding pain, would pace the hallways of the parsonage, up and back, up and back, fingers stroking the wallpaper as she walked, Henry or Flora trailing along behind her. When the riptide of aching returned, Henry and Flora took turns again, rubbing her back, feeding her chips of ice, tamping her forehead with a cool cloth.

The darkness began to succumb to the light of day. Writhing back and forth in the sweat soaked nightclothes, Laura didn't even notice the change. She was fully in the grips of the wild urges of her body. The struggle was upon her, and she felt herself giving up, weakening. Her eyes begging Henry and then Flora, "no more, no more," though those words were never spoken aloud.

At last as evening was arriving once again, exhausted beyond measure, the head of the baby was beginning to crown. This was the moment Flora Bean was waiting for. She would be able to present this new blessed tiny human to, first, this loving and deserving couple, who she had grown so fond of, but also to her church family. It would be a proud moment.

"Okay Mrs. Brooks, are you ready for this? You are about to meet your baby."

Chapter 7:

"...And resembles sorrow only, As the mist resembles rain."

Laura was feverish, defeated, and soaking wet from pushing. For hours now she had pushed on Flora's command, and yet, the baby was not making any progress.

Flora Bean had seen this before. It was a first baby. This was not completely unusual; however, a certain, peculiar uneasiness kept washing over Flora. A nagging haze of worry began to fog her thinking, but she kept pushing the anxious thoughts away as she continued to encourage Laura not to give up.

Flora had quite successfully pushed those thoughts away, right up until bright red tributaries of blood, spilled over her fingers as she examined Mrs. Brooks. She pushed back on her stool. It took a split second for Flora to acknowledge this most urgent disaster before her. She regained her breath, and with one fluid motion rose up from the stool, wiped her crimson hands on her apron and hollered down to Reverend Brooks. In the corner of her eye, she saw the beautiful minister's wife, countenance pale as the face of a new moon, fighting to remain conscious.

"Reverend Brooks," she hollered until he appeared at the foot of the stairs, unkempt with sleeplessness and fretting. "Go now. Go now. Get Dr. Miller. Tell him it is an emergency. He is just over the railroad tracks."

Henry's face flushed with fear and, without hesitation, he fled out the door, and onto his bicycle.

Flora returned to the bedroom and grabbed some rags which had been folded and prepared for the delivery. She pushed them between Laura's legs to quell the bleeding. The crimson outline blossomed into gruesome patterns within seconds straight through the stacked rags. Flora prayed silently, *"Hurry, for the love of all that is good and holy, hurry Reverend."* She looked back at Laura's face, eyes rolling in and out of the stupor of unconsciousness, her head tossing back and forth on her drenched pillowcase. Flora chastised herself silently for waiting so long.

Chapter 8:

"The best thing we can do when it's raining, is to let it rain."

Reverend Brooks careened, off kilter, screeching around the corner between Main and Park Street and over the railroad tracks. He jumped off his bike, leaving it behind as the tires were still spinning round. His bike dropped onto the lawn of the gray cape house belonging to Dr. Miller, with its finely manicured hedges, and breathlessly he ran onto the front porch and pounded on the door with uncommon and desperate forcefulness.

He could hear barking dogs, and a thick German accent scolding the hounds. A distinguished looking gentleman calmly opened the door and he could see he had come at dinnertime. Even in his state of panic, he observed four well mannered children surrounding the dinner table and the strong and unfamiliar, foreign scents of knockwurst and sauerkraut overwhelmed the young minister.

Reverend Brooks frantically found himself thinking, how could they be sitting and eating dinner, when my Laura is dying? My unborn child is dying? And yet, isn't this the reality of the world. Tragedy simultaneously happens for one while the rest of the world remains just as it is.

"Reverend Brooks," Gunther Miller greeted Henry with curiosity, "what brings you..." but mid-sentence he was jolted by the way Reverend Brooks looked. He knew then. "Is it your wife? Is she all right?"

"No, no, please come," Henry Brooks begged, but he needn't have. Dr. Miller was already instructing his wife Ilse, who functioned at times as his nurse, to come with him. He sternly instructed his children to eat their dinner and clean up the dishes. There was no room for questioning.

Grabbing his bag of instruments, he told Reverend Brooks to throw his bicycle into the boot of his car, and jump in. His wife, clearly not dressed for this intrusion to her day, in a day dress and heels, seriously nodded to the minister as she ran, without hesitation, to join her husband for this house call.

Dr. Miller and his wife were Jewish immigrants from Germany. In a hurry to become "American-ized" they moved to Maine and, along with their four children, joined the United Methodist Church, attempting to shed all signs of their Jewish heritage out of fear, still laden deeply, from the persecution of their people and the war.

They were an accomplished and extraordinarily handsome couple in this small Maine town. Their accents, his profession, their lovely home and car...together, all of these made them local celebrities within their community. Reverend Brooks noticed his congregation appeared to adore and revere the family. He felt a certain comfort that the doctor and his wife would take good care of his child and Laura. Everything would be okay.

Chapter 9:

"Every man has secret sorrows, which the world knows not."

The doctor and his wife ran up the front steps of the parsonage, past Laura's carefully tended flower pots, and threw open the door. They didn't wait for invitation as they bolted up the staircase in the center of the house, following the sounds of faceless moans and deep guttural groans. Ilse startled at the sight of the blood soaked rags at the foot of the bed. Gunther didn't hesitate for a single moment to move into action.

"You vill be all right Laura. I vill take gut care of you," he said as he swooped her up into his arms. She hung lifelessly in and out of any awareness, like a rag doll, limp from pain, eyes widening with fear.

Gunther began to head down the stairs with her in his strong arms. His wife, Ilse, ran just ahead, anticipating his needs and clearing off the large dining room table.

Reverend Brooks looked terrified. Flora tossed a sheet on the surface of the table, and Gunther said, "Ve need sie firm table in case I must operate." And at that, Dr. Miller placed Laura on the table as softly as a dove, and Henry was surprised to watch the doctor gently kiss the top of Laura's forehead.

Flora looked exhausted and defeated standing next to Dr. Miller. She remained present in the event that she could be helpful, but her face showed her emotion and grave fear and her eyes were dark and hollow. She stood shakily in her blood stained apron.

Dr. Miller went right to work, moving himself in between Laura's legs as Ilse soaked a cloth with liquid from an amber bottle, and then placed the drenched cloth over Laura's nose and mouth and had her breathe deeply in. Laura's eyes rolled back in her head, and she surrendered to the deep sleep brought on by the ether.

Reverend Brooks felt panicked as he saw the giant metal forceps being brought out of the black leather bag that sat next to his unconscious wife. The tool looked like it had two giant spoons on the end of a scissors handle. It looked as if it were meant more for picking up logs in a river jam than for pulling out the tender head of an infant. "Before ve operate, ve must try forceps. Zis baby must come out quickly," and Reverend Brooks felt the icy hand of Flora on his shoulder, concern shrouding her face like a veil.

The forceps disappeared between Laura's legs and Dr. Miller grimaced and pulled, Ilse at his side, holding back Laura's lifeless legs. The strength he had to use to pull, was so impossibly violent. Reverend Brooks stooped at the waist, unable to believe his child's head was within the grip of this instrument. Dr. Miller braced a leg to the side of the table to strengthen his grip, and with a deep grunt, he pulled. It seemed it would tear the baby's head from its neck.

"Almost, almost, come on, come on," Dr. Miller gave one pull with all of his strength, and there he was, clamped in the jaws of the forceps, a baby. Ilse grabbed the lifeless blue little boy and handed him to Flora. Dr. Miller went to work on Laura, deftly moving between her knees, sewing, blotting, clotting, sweating, working, while Flora went to work on the boy.

Reverend Brooks was dazed, not knowing where to fix his glance. His dining room had taken on the appearance of a night-marish, makeshift operating room in the midst of a field of battle.

Chapter 10:

"And often times we call a man cold, when he is only sad."

Henry leaned over his infant son, praying he would hear a sound. He had to avert his eyes from his son's misshapen head, dented and bruised in the temples, from the force of the tool used to pull him into the world. But he lay there, tiny wrinkled fingers and hands seeming to reach into the air, blue and still and completely silent. Flora, beads of sweat lining her forehead, spoke to the baby hoarsely, pleading urgently, "Come on now, come on now little boy, little one," dabbing cold water on his little face, flicking his impossibly small feet with a snap of her fingers.

Quite suddenly with an unexpected ferocity, Flora plucked up his little form and flipped him upside down. *Thwack.* She swatted his tiny wee bum bringing forth the sharp intake of air, and then, blessedly, the sound of crying. *Blessed be the sound,* thought Reverend Brooks. *My son, my son, the sound of my beautiful son. Thank you Lord.* Henry cast his eyes upward, and then looked directly at his boy, blurred, through tear-filled and tender eyes, painfully accepting the sight of his son's damaged skull, as long as his son was alive. Come what may.

Flora seemed to have the crisis well in hand, so the reverend quickly turned his attention to his wife, dear Laura. Blood soaked towels surrounded Dr. Miller's feet.

The doctor worked urgently, directing his own capable wife to hand him this, hand him that, "more sponges, now thread."

Laura's palor was gray. Her lips were blue tinged. Reverend Brooks felt his legs buckle. Ilse saw this out of the corner of her eye. "Sit now," she commanded firmly, and she turned right back to work at her husband's elbow. Henry sat, holding his spinning head in his hands.

Seconds, minutes, was it hours that had passed? Henry remained sitting, helpless and shocked at what was happening all around him. And then, Flora appeared next to him, with a tiny baby, all cleaned up and wrapped in a powder blue, hand knit blanket, a tiny soft cap placed on his bruised head.

"Would you like a turn at holding this little fellow?" she crooned as she placed the tightly swaddled child into his arms. Dazed, he held out his arms and took in the warm bundle. His son.

Reverend Brooks looked up at Flora, searching her face, "Will he, will he," he stammered.

Flora understood what he was asking, "He had a rough entrance into this world, but he is here, and isn't he a beauty?"

And he was. He was a handsome boy. Closing his eyes to the light, tiny fists twisting into his little bird mouth, Reverend Brooks held him gently, this tiny stranger. With the weight of this little baby in his arms, he silently and steadily prayed for Laura, repeating "thy will be done, thy will be done," thinking only that the Lord's will would be to keep this baby's mother alive to care for him.

"Thy will be done," he said aloud, and turned to see Dr. and Mrs. Miller, who hours ago had been sitting at the dinner table, blood stained, weary, their faces marked with relief.

"Bring zat darlink little boy over to his Mamma," Ilse said, smiling softly, moving to Laura's bedside.

She leaned in to whisper, "You vill be fine, Laura. You have such a handsome baby boy," a tear rolling down her cheek. It was evident the whole event had been nearly as terrifying for her as it had been for Flora and Henry.

Flora, Dr. Miller and his wife, all stepped from the room, an exhausted and relieved team of three, and Reverend Brooks lowered the baby onto Laura's chest. All was well. All was well. Laura and her baby had survived.

Reverend Brooks took in the sight. The color was beginning to return to his wife's beautiful face, and she gently caressed and kissed the little tiny boy in her arms. He heard Laura crooning softly in her son's ear.

"Norman," she said in a hoarse whisper. "Little Norman." And she placed a light kiss right on Norman's little lips.

Henry's hands were still trembling. He looked before him and wondered at her beauty even after all she had been through. Her gaze remained fixed on their new son. How could he have been so blessed? He silently gave thanks to the Lord, as he moved toward her. And even years later, he remembered the exact moment that he heard his wife say, "Henry, Henry," and he met her eyes with his own, "he's just so perfect."

Chapter 11:

The horrible scare the new minister and his wife experienced took no time to spread through the town of Livermore. One by one, the tale was told and retold about the ordeal. Dozens of casseroles were baked, money was collected, care packages assembled.

Dr. Miller made several more house calls, as was the practice in the day, to be sure Laura was back on her feet, and healing. As it turned out, she had experienced a placental abruption, a true and rare medical emergency during delivery. Dr. Miller credited Flora and Reverend Brooks for their quick thinking, immediately sending for a doctor. Any hesitation, he believed, would have ended in a complete and utter catastrophe. Surely hesitating to call for help would have resulted in the death of one or both of the fortunate pair, mother and son.

The ladies of the congregation began to arrive, knocking nervously, at the door of the parsonage. Naturally, Flora took charge. She ushered each in for a quick little peek at the baby. She would accept and label each dish being delivered so as not to confuse Laura when it was time to return the empty container. Flora deftly arranged each homemade offering either on the sideboard, in the freezer or in the icebox. Soon the house was filled with steaming pots of goulash, pot roasts, baskets of homemade sweet breads, jelled salads, bread and butter pickles, and hearty meaty stews. She allowed exactly one hour of visits each afternoon, and insisted Laura rest and recuperate for the remainder of the day.

Laura, even with all of the extra help and rest, found herself close to tears and flustered much of the time. Still sore and exhausted from her unexpectedly dramatic and frightening medical ordeal, she believed she would settle right into motherhood. But it was not nearly as simple as that.

Nursing did not come easily. Flora positioned and re-positioned little Norman, but he would barely latch on. Her breasts were full and hardened with milk. Her nipples were raw and searing hot with infection, pasted with healing ointments. She tried over and over again to get Norman to suckle. He just didn't seem interested in nursing, lying listlessly in her arms as she attempted to entice him to drink. She was nearly beside herself.

Her nether-regions were stitched up from "stem to stern" Flora would say. Twice daily she placed a basin filled with hot water on the toilet seat and she would sit in the hot water filled with a combination of baking soda and salt to hurry along healing, but the stitches and the burning in her crotch, in combination with her cracked and oozing nipples, made her feel depressed and revolting.

Flora sensed Laura's defeat and loss of confidence and proposed trying something different for a few feedings. She marched into the kitchen and swiftly turned a church key, deftly prying open a can of evaporated milk. She poured some thick Karo syrup into a pan, added water, and boiled it up on the stovetop. She used an eyedropper to drip some of the sweet mix into Norman's little open mouth. He gurgled and coughed and pushed it away with his tongue, but soon he appeared to settle down and begin to swallow the sweetness. Laura wept with relief.

"There, there Mrs. Brooks," Flora clucked. "There's always more than one way to skin a cat. It will all work itself out. Norman just has his own ideas," she winked, and then looking down at the little brown-eyed boy, "don't you Norman...don't you sweet boy."

Eventually Norman began taking his sweet, milky mixture from a glass baby bottle. This gave Laura a much needed chance to rest. Henry rocked his little boy, feeding him during the day so his wife could nap and gain her strength. Laura had twinges of guilt, wishing she could feed Norman from her own breasts, but Flora helped to push those thoughts away. Within weeks, this new schedule found the young couple coping very nicely, and establishing a fine new routine. Naturally little Norman became the center of their universe.

The purple and green bruising on the sides of Norman's temples slowly faded and with the diminishing signs of injury, Laura and Henry began to relax more and more about the health of their little boy. The terrifying night of the delivery began to feel like a story that happened to someone else, another family.

Chapter 12:

Within a month, Laura was ready to bring Norman to church for Sunday service. Once Henry had left the house in his black robe, draped in his prayer shawl, Laura scurried around to get the baby ready for his first outing. What could be better than surrounding him by his church family for his first public event? Laura was giddy with the excitement of presenting him to the congregation.

Laura pinned him into a fresh cotton diaper and covered it up with a little pair of rubber pants. Oh! Norman was such a handsome little boy. He was so serious with his big brown eyes and somber forehead. And so good, my goodness he was a darling. Once in a while, when he was wet or needed his bottle, he would emit a tiny fuss, but mostly he was quiet, just looking about, taking in his whole world. Oh how she loved her little bundle! She could hardly wait for Ma and Pa to see their handsome bit of a grandson. Soon she and Henry would have to make a trip to Walker Hill. They were surely ready to travel now!

The previous week, Laura had been so delighted when the mailman delivered a parcel addressed from Ma and Pa. Inside of the brown paper wrapping was a tiny handmade blue sailor suit for Norman. That was exactly what he would wear for his first visit to church.

Laura snapped on the little blue suit, admiring each of Ma's even and perfect teensy stitches. She knew this was made with love in every pull of the thread. She placed a handsome blue bonnet onto Norman's head, covering the nearly unnoticeable remains of the yellow and green bruising, and tied a bow beneath his chin. She bundled Norman up in a cream blanket she had knit herself, and placed him gently into his carriage. Grabbing her handbag, and a bag with Norman's diapers and bottles, they strolled next door, pulled in by the familiar sounds of the pipe organ.

The ushers pushed open the door, their faces registering their clear and obvious delight in seeing the minister's wife and child in attendance. Laura had regained her statuesque figure remarkably quickly after the birth of Norman. The first couple of weeks, she was so weak and exhausted, she had little appetite, so the pounds she had gained during her pregnancy fell off effortlessly. She had taken particular care with her appearance on this important morning, so she knew she looked quite lovely as she passed the ushers with a radiant smile and polite nod.

Laura parked the stroller in the entryway of the church and plucked up little Norman, proudly walking him down the aisle to her seat, next to, an absolutely thrilled, Flora in the front pew of the church. She could feel the warm embrace of her church family behind her. Flora gave her a little wink, feeling ever so proud of all she had contributed to the well being of this special little family.

Chapter 13:

The tiny blonde acolyte proudly held the brushed brass candle lighter, the flame dancing to and fro as she made her way toward the candles she had the job of lighting this morning. She was dressed in a Swiss dotted pink dress, her hair tied back neatly in a tiny pigtail. She led Reverend Brooks down the aisle. She paused at the altar, bowing deeply, carefully following the exact directions of the ushers. This gave Reverend Brooks a good chance to stop and take in the beauty of his son and wife on the front pew.

It nearly took his breath to see them both. Laura had never looked more radiant. She wore just barely a hint of make up, her hair was a neatly arranged mass of shining curls, her mouth in a perpetual smile, looking down at sweet Norman. His heart was full and brimming with gratitude.

The acolyte completed her task of lighting the altar candles. She smiled proudly, her gaze searching for her parents in the congregation, before descending the stairs, carefully snuffing out the candle lighter. Her task had been a complete success.

Reverend Brooks took his place behind the altar and opened his hymnal. "Let's all turn to page 238 and together raise our voices to sing *Holy, Holy, Holy*," he said smiling down at his wife. He knew this was one of her favorite hymns. She knowingly caught his eye, blushing slightly with the secret between them.

The organist played the refrain once through, and then commenced to the beginning of the hymn, as the congregation began, "Holy, holy, holy, Lord God almighty..."

Laura raised her voice. Although she was unable to carry little Norman and hold her hymnal, there was no need. She knew every word by heart. Singing filled her heart with joy, and as she sang, she closed her eyes imagining holding hands around the table up on Walker Hill, singing this song with her family before eating their evening meal. She couldn't wait to return there, with little Norman in tow. How he would love the hills, the farm, the animals, the fields and the ponds.

"World without end, amen, amen," the song ended on a lovely drawn out note, and the congregation began to sit in unison.

As Laura took her seat, her breath caught in her throat. She felt Norman's little body tensing strangely in her arms. Her heart quickened as she felt his body go rigid. Panic swelled in her chest, and although no words were exchanged, Flora sensed somehow that something was wrong. She moved toward Laura on the pew. This unusual commotion caught Henry's attention, and mid-sentence, he stopped.

Norman began convulsing in Laura's arms. Laura stood up, wild-eyed...her little boy's limbs thrashing, an animalistic chortling rose from deep within his throat. Norman's back arched strangely, his eyes rolled back until Laura could see only the whites, his big brown unseeing eyes disappearing beneath his lids. Flora stretched her arms out to take Norman into her own.

Laura's primitive motherly instinct swelled within her and she would not hand her baby to another woman. She ran toward her husband, who by then had run down from the pulpit to his wife and infant son. Laura all but threw Norman toward him, wordlessly, her eyes pleaded for Henry to do something.

Dr. Miller and his wife were among the congregation, and right away knew something was quite wrong. They guessed it was the baby. The members of the congregation, hushed with what was happening in front of them, watched nervously as Dr. Miller made his way toward the couple. "Normy, Normy," the Reverend was saying, "come little boy. Come now," but Norman's limbs still were stiffened and the horrible guttural sound continued to rise from his throat. His body felt colder through his wraps and his lips tinged a shade of blue.

Dr. Miller grabbed the baby from his father's arms, and laid him down on the carpeted church floor, and told everyone to step back. "He's having a seizure," he said to whomever was listening, "he vill stop, he vill stop." Over and over, he repeated the words in his German accent, "he vill stop…," a mantra meant to soothe, meant to will the cruel grips of the seizure to cease.

Was it minutes? Was it hours? How long was it before his seizing stopped? Laura was clutching her husband's arms, leaning over Dr. Miller. Both firmly in the depths of an icy terror, the kind of fear that is incited only when death seems to be hovering near.

Just as incredulously as the seizure had entered the room, it exited without warning. Suddenly, the tiny baby, exhausted from his convulsing, fell into a deep sleep. Limp as a dishrag, Dr. Miller scooped him up, put his ear to the baby's tiny chest, and satisfied with what he heard, he handed him back to his terrified father.

Both Laura and the Reverend stood in shock, huddled around their boy, not knowing what had just taken place. They somberly walked to the back of the church, following Dr. Miller, leaving the congregation agog behind them.

Laura thought she heard the din of prayer in their wake, but perhaps the prayer was only in her mind.

Chapter 14:

Dr. Miller knew the little family didn't have their own car, so he rose early to drive Laura and Henry to the bus station in his shiny, black DeSoto. They had packed a modest overnight bag, and in the wee hours of the morning, with the sun just cresting over their little town, they stood shivering on the platform at the bus station to go to Boston, Massachusetts. Their faces were somber, as he pulled away from the station, but Dr. Miller reminded them the best doctors in the world were in Boston, and Boston was exactly where they should be.

Bumping along in the huge Greyhound bus, side by side in the very front seat behind the driver, their eyes kept moving between their soundly sleeping baby and the horizon. The huge windshield in front of them reflected their images. Their worried faces revealed the terror that was churning inside of them.

Laura had never been out of the state of Maine before. As a girl she imagined that once she crossed the state line into New Hampshire, it would be a spectacular moment. As the bus crested the biggest bridge either Laura or Henry had ever seen, from Maine into Portsmouth, New Hampshire, there was no joy, only fear. The occasion for which she left the state, allowed no room for awe whatsoever.

They had an 11:00 appointment with a children's neurologist. Dr. Miller had arranged for Norman to be seen at the Boston Children's Hospital. Since that fateful day at church, they had run to his office many times, a writhing baby in their arms, fearful beyond words that he would die. Dr. Miller recognized the limitations of his small practice and contacted his colleagues in Boston. He explained that the doctors there would be able to look inside of Norman's brain. They could see what inside of Norman's head was causing these horrific seizures.

So, they were on their way. Laura pressed her forehead to the cool window next to her, and silently prayed that they would find a cure for the little boy in her arms. Although she had not had a lot of practice with babies, so she had relatively few babies to compare Norman against, she wondered about his development. She questioned Flora often. "Shouldn't he be rolling over by now?" Laura would fret.

Flora would coo and cluck over little Norman, and say reassuringly, "Oh you know he had a harsh entry into this world. He will do things in his own time, in his own way," but her words did precious little to bring Laura comfort. She would stare at him lying on his back, willing him to attempt to roll. Laura would shake a little rattle to his left or to his right, but as often as not, Norman would ignore the sound, neither turning his head nor rolling in its direction.

"Do other babies smile by now?" she would ask, brow furrowed with concern.

The nagging voice never left Laura's mind. Norman was so quiet. Once in a great while, he would fuss a bit, but with no rhyme or reason attached to his noises. It wasn't at predictable times like when his diaper was full or when he was hungry. And he never deliberately smiled or laughed out of glee. Sometimes, as Laura looked into his eyes as she was spooning custard into his mouth, he would stare right at her. Her heart melted at the thought of receiving a gummy smile from him. But he would gaze, seemingly, right through her. He was such a still and serious little fellow.

But his stern little face was that of an angel. He had downy soft fawn colored hair, with giant chocolate brown eyes, and skin as soft as rose petals. Laura and Henry watched over him like hawks. They spent hours trying to make him smile, to coo, and they would watch for him to get angry and cry...but he remained still and quiet, except for when he was seizing.

His seizures were so violent. The episodes entered his body like an earthquake, erupting into each limb firing from his core. It was then that he made noise. His back jerked into an impossible arch. Horrible gurgling, throaty churning, gasping sounds haunted his parents deep into the night. They slept fitfully, if and when they slept, with a constant ear to the bassinet, with one hand resting on his back as he slumbered. They waited.

Riding to Boston, Henry and Laura were distracted by their worries. Back and forth, they would take turns cradling little Norman. Each would bend to kiss his warm forehead, pat his back, stroke his cheek.   Deep and persistent worry, their constant unwelcome companion, never left their side.

Henry put his arm around his wife's shoulder, and she laid her head against his woolen coat.   The traffic began to thicken. Horns blared, and the bus jolted to and fro, starting and stopping at lights and turns. The brick buildings were taller than either Laura or Henry had ever seen. Curious to see the city they had read and heard so much about, they took in all of the noise and unfamiliar sights of Boston streaking past from their bus window.

So many windows in the tall brick structures. There were hundreds upon hundreds of windows in each building.   Laura wondered if, within each window, young mothers had bouncing baby boys and cooing baby girls rolling about in their walkers, banging their spoons on their high chairs.

She wondered if perhaps within one of those windows, there was a mother such as herself. Holding a baby with no expression. Holding a baby with no movements other than violent, jerking, horrible movements. She turned her head away from the buildings. The bus rolled on.

Chapter 15:

They arrived at the bus station, and stepped nervously into this unknown land. It was so noisy. Blaring horns, screeching brakes, the sounds of the city creating a riotous, unfamiliar clatter. Laura felt tempted to cover her ears and Norman's too. She glanced sideways at Henry who was following Dr. Miller's very specific instructions on "how to hail a taxicab". He looked nervous, uncomfortable, such a country mouse in the big city.

Once in the backseat of the cab, Henry instructed the driver to take his little family to Boston Children's Hospital. The driver appeared surprised. Little Norman really was a beautiful baby, and perhaps to others he looked the picture of health. But deep within the folds of his brain, his parents knew, without a doubt, he was badly damaged.

As they pulled into the huge hospital's intimidating entrance, Henry reached into his wallet to hand the driver cash for the lift. The driver waved the money away. Both Henry and Laura were deeply touched by the gesture, and Henry tried to insist. The driver said in his distinct Bostonian accent, "Just take care of that there baby mistah." Henry nodded gratefully, sliding the bills back into his billfold, as the driver pulled back into the maze of traffic.

Chapter 16:

The journey to get to the hospital was long. Four hours all told. However, once they were in the hospital, things moved quite quickly. To Henry and Laura, it felt too fast. Almost immediately, a lovely young red headed nurse, in a perfectly pinned white nursing cap tipped back on her head, took Norman from a reluctant Laura's arms. Laura could feel the weight of her baby long after he had been whisked away.

They both watched as this efficient nurse weighed and measured little Norman. She placed him in a plastic bassinet, clucking at him sweetly, and then wrote things deftly onto the sheets of her clipboard. She prodded him a bit, here and there, the bottom of his bare foot, in the dimple of his knee, and again she grabbed her clipboard and wrote things down. Laura wondered what she was writing.

She turned him on his tummy, and took his rectal temperature. Still, even with such an invasive and unpleasant intrusion, he made no sounds. Laura felt the nurse certainly must be writing notes about the fact that he was silent, and this made her feel irrational, defensive and edgy. She fought the urge to go and grab him.

Once the red headed nurse was finished with her assessment of Norman, she handed him back to a very eager Laura and then rapid-fire began to ask questions. Questions about his birth that made the young couple shudder with the memories.

As the questions were answered, she would write their replies in her coded shorthand.

"Tell me about his sleep habits," she asked, and as Laura began to answer, she could feel the familiar tensing of Norman's limbs. The nurse's trained eye immediately picked up that there was an issue, and reached for Norman. Henry and Laura both paled as she placed Norman in the bassinet and rang for help. Through the transparent sides of the hospital bassinet, they watched the familiar arc of Norman's back, the telltale pre-cursor of his seizures.

Doctors and nurses flooded the room, each with a clear role in their response to this medical situation, as Norman convulsed in front of this new audience. As Henry and Laura wrenched their necks around the growing cluster of medical staff, they were ushered from the room by some non-descript member of the team responding to Norman. They had never been apart from Norman during a seizure, and all of their instincts told them to fight to be there for their baby, but, obediently, they both did as they were told.

The dazed young couple were led to a sterile, beige waiting room. A glass pitcher of water sat in the center of the coffee table. Henry instinctively walked in and poured a glass for Laura who was as white as a sheet. She could see his hand visibly quaking as he poured the water. Laura gratefully accepted the glass, and sat on the olive cushioned chair, eyes glancing the Bible on the table. She noticed Henry reaching for it, and then changing his mind, simply sitting back on his chair deeply sighing, his hands folded behind his head.

There was no sense of how much time had passed. Finally, a doctor wearing a long white coat, mask hanging from around his neck, entered the waiting room with the same red headed nurse who had first greeted them. Both Henry and Laura rose to their feet. He asked them to please sit back down, and he wearily sat himself opposite from them.

It was then that they learned their son had temporal lobe epilepsy. The doctor hypothesized that the damage sustained by the necessary use of forceps during his traumatic delivery was causing Norman's severe epileptic seizures. Both Laura and Henry, in the quiet of their own minds, knew long before being told by a Bostonian doctor, that their son's violent birth had most certainly caused his health challenges. Now, it was simply confirmed.

The doctor suggested that Norman would be a strong candidate for a new surgery that was being tested on patients with epilepsy. He explained that he would carve a half moon into Norman's tiny skull and remove the lesion, the damaged part of Norman's brain, eliminating his horrible seizures. Laura reached for Henry's ice cold hand as the doctor drew out, on a sheet of paper, how he would go into Norman's brain and cut out the damaged tissue, ultimately stopping the dangerous and frequent seizures.

What were they to say? This was what had to be done. Who were they to question these fine surgeons? The best in the world, they were told.

The surgery was scheduled for the next morning. Laura and Henry both nodded, trusting simply that the doctors did, indeed, know best. Although as the doctor turned to leave the room, Laura did stammer out one question hesitantly. "Doctor, will Norman be, well, will he be...normal, after this surgery?"

The doctor answered only, "Well, he should have no more seizures after his surgery."

Laura stood waiting, still, wanting her question to be answered. "But, will he be normal," she repeated.

He answered only, "Time will tell."

The nurse handed Norman back to his young mother. Laura raised the familiar weight of him to her lips, and kissed him ever so gently on the forehead. Time would tell.

Chapter 17:

It had been a harrowing and exhausting two weeks for Henry and Laura, but

fourteen days from the day they arrived, they had little Norman back in their arms

and in their keeping. They stood on the very same ramp in the station, in the dank,

exhaust- filled air, waiting to take the bus back to their home in Livermore.

Just as the doctors had warned, Norman had an angry half moon scar on his left

temple. The jagged gash such an unwelcome interruption to his lovely face. The

doctors felt certain they had removed the lesion causing the seizures, so in addition

to the bags they carried, they left holding optimism that their baby would fully

recover. Norman had not had one seizure following his operation!

Following their four hour ride back to Maine, Flora greeted the little threesome at

the bus station. They were so pleased to see her. She closely examined little

Norman, peeking beneath his bonnet, and "tut-tut-tuting" at his scar. Afterwards,

she swiftly hopped behind the steering wheel. Laura found herself amused and

fascinated by the competence of this sturdy little woman. The hands that pulled

babies into the world also were fully capable of driving and shifting a car. Laura

knew very few women who were able to drive.

The majestic autumnal greens and golds of the countryside outside of the car

window were a welcome contrast to the noisy chaos of the city. It was lovely to see the beginnings of fall. The tips of maple leaves were beginning to boast reds, oranges, and yellows. Fall in Maine, arguably the most beautiful season, was upon them. The crisp air, coupled with having Norman's surgery behind them, filled Henry and Laura with renewed spirits and hope.

As could have been predicted, the parsonage pantry and icebox were completely filled with food. The members of the church were, once again, generous with their giving, and they carefully divided the task of providing for the Reverend and his family among all of the church families. As they unpacked from their time in Boston, they realized they wanted for nothing in their little home. They had fresh milk, eggs, cream and breads, casseroles, bowls of fruit and homemade sweets, teas and coffees. It was good to be home.

Once little Norman was tucked into his bassinet for the night, Laura fussed around in her kitchen, placing all of the items back into each of the proper spots. Henry put a teakettle on the stovetop to boil, and prepared two cups for English tea. The ordinary felt extraordinary considering their last two difficult weeks with Norman.

Cup in hand, Henry retired to his study. He opened his Bible and put a blank piece of paper before him. The experience they had just been through should provide plenty of adequate fodder for an inspirational sermon this Sunday, he thought. The gratitude he felt for the sure hands of the surgeons, the grace he experienced at arriving home to a house full of provisions, and the hope he held in his heart for his son's recovery...all of these examples of God at work in the form of people, he believed would bring forth real kernels of life to preach about.

Laura went about her business, tidying and sorting and arranging her little nest, her quaint and lovely parsonage. She felt so grateful for the comforting, familiar smells and sounds, and tastes of home. She peeked in, every few minutes, on Norman. He slumbered soundly in his crib. His tiny fists were balled up against each side of his face. The sound of his quiet breathing was music to her ears. All was well in their one tiny corner of the world.

Hours later, however, Henry's paper remained blank in front of him.

Chapter 18:

Autumn became winter. Winter melted into spring.

Norman's toes began pushing their way out of his cotton sleepers. He grew longer

and he filled out until his cheeks were even a bit plump. He seemed to enjoy his food

more than ever. Thankfully, his seizures had stopped. However, Norman was ever

still. Ever quiet.

When Laura pulled him to his feet in her lap, he wouldn't brace his legs to stand as

she saw other babies do. When she placed him on his belly, he merely remained in

place, head tipped to one side of the other, never attempting to push himself up on

his arms, or flip his little body over.

If and when he smiled, it was merely a fluke. But, oh how Laura loved to see his face

light up. She would pray for it at night. However, his face did not light up when she

walked into the room from his nap, and he didn't reach for her when she bent to

pick him up. He didn't hold his bottle; he didn't reach for his spoon.

Week after week, Laura would bring him to the front pew of the church for his

father's services. He would sit in her lap, still and silent, and Flora and the other

church ladies would make of him. Laura would put on a brave front. She would dress him up, get him all ready, but there was no mistaking and there was no hiding that something wasn't right.

Other little babies of the church, much younger than Norman, were cooing and fussing and kicking up fits, standing in their mother's laps. Each of the children, born well after Norman, was quickly doing all of the things Laura was anxiously waiting for. They would coo, and giggle, and reach, and clap, and stand, and crawl, and bounce in the laps of their mothers.

Admittedly, it was hard to watch. Laura tried very hard not to compare Norman to the other babies. She just focused on him and his gentle, quiet spirit. But Laura could see her husband begin to pull away from the babies of the church. He used to reach for them, and playfully tug at their ears. Recently, Henry seemed changed. He was cold as mothers and fathers would greet him at the end of his sermons.

Laura stood next to him as the receiving line passed, and she would see babies reach their chubby fingers out to grab at her husband's robe. Henry would turn away, disinterested. Mothers, embarrassed, would awkwardly move past, pulling their babies toward their chests, grabbing their little fingers away from the disdainful face of the minister.

In the evenings, Laura would feed and bathe and then change Norman for bed. She would warm his bottle, as she had for months, for Henry to give him his nighttime feeding before putting Norman in his crib. Henry used to beam as she handed over their clean and sleepy boy, quietly humming their favorite Methodist hymns, Rock of Ages or Amazing Grace, as he rocked his boy to sleep. Recently, however, Henry began making excuses, night after night, of why he was too busy for the nightly ritual, until, over time, Laura eventually stopped asking and rocked him to sleep on her own.

"Lord give me the strength to accept that which I cannot change," Laura would whisper again and again in prayer, gripping her beautiful son to her chest, closing her eyes against tears that would not be quelled. "Thy will be done," but why was this God's will, she questioned burrowing her face in her son's soft, fragrant hair.

Chapter 19:

Laura strapped Norman into his wheelchair. The new leather strap buckled around his chest to help hold him upright. Even after doing exercises meant to strengthen his trunk, he always listed to the right, sometimes tipping over. She hated when ugly knots would appear on his forehead indicating he had bumped his head without her knowing.

Laura popped a smart looking cap on his head, and pushed his wheelchair toward the church. It wasn't easy. She now had one newborn baby girl in a stroller, and Norman in a wheelchair. She deftly put the brakes on the baby stroller and wheeled Norman up the ramp and into the vestry. The ushers readily watched Norman, as was their customary routine, while Laura ran to quickly grab her baby in order to stroll her into church as well. The ushers exchanged empathic looks, recognizing how full Mrs. Brooks' hands always seemed to be.

Flora, now walking, completely annoyed and reluctantly, with the assistance of a cane, slid her self over on the pew to mind Norman for Laura. She was clearly frustrated to have to use the cane, and placed it next to her seat with a decided "humph" and a certain, unmistakable degree of hostility. Laura wordlessly parked Norman's chair next to Flora's seat in the front pew, and ran back down the aisle to get her beautiful, plump and healthy, brunette baby girl, Rose.

Breathlessly, Laura settled into her pew, baby in arms. The organ music began to play, and Laura turned, exhaling from her busy morning preparations, just as her husband was walking down the center of the church, following closely behind a little be-spectacled and serious acolyte. Henry looked incredibly thin and pale she thought. His hands, holding the Holy Bible, were visibly shaking.

Seeing the frailty of her husband, startled Laura suddenly. Between feeding, changing, and tending both Norman and the new baby, Laura was trying to remember. Had Henry been eating? She never had time to prepare, sit and eat a meal herself. She was nursing little Rose and most of the time, while she did so, she was using the other hand to spoon food into Norman's waiting mouth, or was putting a cup to his lips so he would take sips in between his bites.

Generally, Laura ate standing up or in fits and starts. Never did she have an entire meal from start to finish. When Rose was first born, Ma and Pa came to Livermore for a blessed two weeks. Aunt Hildy dropped them off in the driveway, each with a small satchel in hand, and Ma with a basket filled with her fresh baked goods. Their arrival was a gift straight from heaven. That was the last time Laura could remember sitting down for a meal.

Pa would sit and happily rock the baby in the study, humming a familiar hymn, or quietly reciting poetry.

"Kind hearts are the gardens, Kind thoughts are the roots, Kind words are the flowers,

Kind deeds are the fruits."

Ma would be in the kitchen most of the afternoon preparing the evening meal. She would bake buttermilk biscuits, rolling the dough out on the counter, standing in a cloud of flour, pressing a round tin cutter through the dough. At the table, she would ladle out steaming stews filled with chunks of root vegetables and savory tender meats.

Henry would eat quietly, perhaps grateful for the sustenance, but with no visible joy. Laura would first blow a spoonful cool for Norman, and then bring a bite to her son's mouth, and then, from the same spoon, take a bite for herself. After dinner, Ma would clean the kitchen until every surface was spotless. Henry would retire to his study, close the door and prepare his sermon. Laura would take the baby from Pa, and modestly nurse beneath a draped afghan. Pa would sit with Norman until the baby was fed and bathed and placed into her cradle. When Laura finished with the baby, she would bathe and diaper Norman and place him in his bed, put up his rail, and return to the tidy living room to visit with Pa and Ma for a few blessed, quiet moments, sipping chamomile tea, before they would all go off to bed.

Days were exhausting, but having Ma and Pa in the house, helping, gave Laura an inner strength. Their support, while there, was unspoken, unwavering and steadfast. Seeing Henry taking his place behind the altar, made Laura painfully recall a moment in time that took place when her parents were visiting.

One evening, while Henry was quietly eating his pot roast dinner, Laura was cutting up Norman's portion into tiny bites. Ma was busying herself in the kitchen, placing rolls, hot from the oven, into a wicker basket. Pa was walking into the study cradling Rose for their evening ritual, and Pa quietly said, in his even baritone voice, "I bet Laura would enjoy a little break from feeding Norman tonight," looking stonily in Henry, his son in law's, direction.

Pa was a man of few words, and he certainly was never a man to interfere outside of his own business. A tangible tension hung in the air, following Pa's pointed suggestion.

Henry just kept eating, not looking up, never acknowledging Pa's words whatsoever. Pa shook his head in obvious disappointment. Ma swooped in quickly to ease the mood and nullify the awkwardness. She nudged at Laura to take over Norman's evening feeding. Laura shook Ma away and said with as much enthusiasm as she could muster, "Oh no Pa. I love to feed Normy. It's never any trouble," and she spooned a bite into Norman's open mouth, her smiling face unsuccessful in masking her disappointed eyes.

Ma quickly bustled to Laura's side refusing to take "no" for an answer. "Now see here Laura. It's my turn tonight," and Laura looked, in spite of her words, relieved to hand over the spoon, and slide over to the next seat. She tried to enjoy her dinner, without having to feed Norman for one evening, but she could not enjoy a single bite.

Henry had pushed his plate aside, and left the table without a word.

Chapter 20:

Henry stood at the altar, and Laura's eyes pooled with tears. Sitting back from the pew, fully and completely taking the time to focus for the moment on her husband, she realized how much he had changed over the years, since Norman's birth. He was thin and his features, once solidly handsome, were now angular and somber. His eyes, once warm and prone to a devilish twinkle, were now removed, distant, and cold. No, not cold. Angry. Angry was a better word.

Her gaze shifted to Norman's face, next to hers. How could his birth harden Henry's heart so? He was such a beautiful boy. The terrifying seizures were gone now, so he was gaining weight and filling out. He had no speech; however, he spoke to Laura in other ways. She tried to tell Henry, he just had to open his heart to really "hear" what Normy was "saying".

When Norman opened his mouth to Laura's feedings, in her mind she would hear him saying, "Yummy, Mommy." When she bathed and diapered him, and lowered him to bed, carefully tucking him into his soft blankets, she would hear, "Good night Mommy." When she gently kissed his warm forehead, she heard him say, "I love you Mommy." She heard all this. She truly did. Not through spoken words, but directly through her heart.

When she told Henry these things, he would harshly dismiss her words and sputter, "Nonsense Laura."

Henry's sermons lacked the same emotion as his life. His words were rote, his prayers were stiff, his sermons were tinged with a palpable anger and bitterness. He used to joyfully raise his baritone voice to the skies when he sang his favorite hymns. His voice could be heard over the entire congregation. No longer. Now, he opened his hymnal, and simply followed along, appearing anxious for each song to come to an end.

Laura continued to try to reach him, as he preached, through her deliberate and familiar nods of encouragement as he spoke. She tried to tease out his personality through her smiles and deliberate eye contact, and through purposeful gazes exchanged throughout the service. When Henry first became a minister, he frequently found his wife's face to gauge her responses throughout the entire service, measuring each and every expression, but now, he very rarely, if ever, even looked her way.

She could tell, through reading the faces of the congregation, once excited and welcoming to Reverend Brooks and his family, they clearly were beginning to feel distant and disconnected from their minister. The receiving line at the end of the service was formal and stiff, a perfunctory task. When the Brooks first came to Livermore, the receiving line would take many minutes to get through. Family after family would stop and exchange anecdotes and swap short stories and laughs. Each wanted their turn with Reverend Brooks.   That was no longer the case. Now they simply shook his hand, "Thank you, pastor," and coolly moved on.

There was no doubt in Laura's mind. They were all losing him. She was losing him. And she had no idea what to do.

Chapter 21:

He just stopped. He just stopped and walked away.

The congregation was mid-sentence in the Lord's Prayer, "On earth as it is in heaven. Give us this day," and then he stopped. Laura's head was bent in prayer. Her baby girl, Rose, was in her arms, when she heard her husband's baritone voice stop leading the prayer.

Instantly alarmed, she looked up to the pulpit to see why he had stopped speaking. He had closed his Bible. He took his glasses off from the perch of his nose and carefully placed them atop the Bible. He steadied himself with one hand, and appeared to take a sharp breath in, and then he walked down the stairs of the altar.

His glance never shifted left or right. His eyes looked straight out the back door of the church.

Laura moved toward him. She reached out to grab his arm as he moved past her, but then she dropped her hand. She instinctively looked toward Flora who stood looking equally perplexed, shaking her head and shrugging her shoulders.

It felt as if the entire congregation were looking at Laura for answers. She stood holding her baby, one hand gripping onto the handle of Norman's wheelchair. She could feel the color rising in her cheeks, tears brimming in her eyes.

Flora, clearly flustered, moved to help with Norman's wheelchair. Laura grabbed the baby's things, and the two of them left the confused congregation behind as they headed to the parsonage. Flora hooked her cane to the back of Norman's chair and pushed his wheelchair to the front door of the parsonage, and left Laura and Henry to their privacy.

Laura almost hoped to discover that Henry was home because he was suddenly taken ill. She hoped to find him in bed or in the bathroom vomiting, or lying on the couch with a cold cloth on his head. She hoped she would see an obvious reason for a grown man to have walked out on his work. Instead, she found him in his study. He was setting up his easel.

She approached him, baby in arms, "Henry, what on earth are you doing?" she asked her voice shrill with worry.

He looked up with an expression of nonchalance. He began squirting big blobs of oil paint onto his palate with great flair and uncharacteristically over exaggerated movements. "Laura," he answered without looking up, a snarky tone evident in his voice, "It appears that I am going to paint." He spat each word out angrily.

Henry frequently painted. His tools were always an arm's length away, wrapped in a cloth roll, kept in his study. He often rewarded himself, once his sermon was completely written, by painting to celebrate his accomplishment. Painting was an outlet that brought Henry incredible solace and light. The parsonage was dotted, throughout, with lovely landscapes and stills. Even the staircase had free hand, primitive and whimsical paintings on the face of each step.

Henry was an artist in many regards. He played the piano by ear. He painted beautifully. He played effortlessly. It gave Laura great joy to watch him completely involved in his artistic endeavors. He appeared transcended, and she frequently envied his ability to experience complete escape. She wished she had the skills and the time to be able to find her own escape, but that wasn't to be. Not with Norman and the baby to care for.

"But Henry," she said, although she suspected it needed not to be stated, "the church. The service. What, what..." she tried to appeal to him, unable to find adequate words to pose her question. She wanted to ask him what the fresh hell he was doing, but as oft happened recently with his unpredictable moodiness, she hesitated to speak so plainly.

"What? What Laura?" he snapped back. "What about them? I. Am. Painting." He punctuated each word with a deep anger and disdain that made Laura shirk backwards. And he did indeed return to his canvas. He looked back at her, an intrusion to his plan, "Leave me to it Laura."

And so she did. She left him to it.

Chapter 22:

Canvas after canvas began to line up. Day after day and into the night, Henry painted like a mad man. One after the other, members of the board of ministry came to see him. Somber men would enter the study, to find a euphoric, disinterested artist frantically painting.

They would try to appeal to him to return to his ministry, his calling, his role in the church. They told him his congregation needed him. They reminded him he was obligated. Eventually, they told him he had a contract.

Laura anxiously would stand outside of the study door as the men entered, listening hopefully to each as they tried to reach Henry somehow. They were gentle and kind. Then they became stern and firm. Neither approach made any difference whatsoever.

One by one, they would leave the study, shutting the door behind. Nervously out in the kitchen, Laura was waiting hopefully, but she could tell immediately, by the defeated look on each deacon and board member's face; their conversation had made no difference.

The men weren't without sensitivity. It was evident to Laura that they felt horrible. Each, filing past as he left the study, could not look away from poor Laura, caring for her crippled son and sweet baby daughter. But at the end of it all, they were paying him to do a job that he was no longer doing. Moreover, they were paying for the parsonage in which they were living.

Laura kept praying. Henry kept painting.

Chapter 23:

Dr. Miller rubbed his forehead as he sat Laura down following his examination of the Reverend. "I believe he is suffering from a severe case of melancholia. Zis is perhaps caused by his extreme feelings of guilt or loss due to Norman's condition." Laura nodded waiting for more answers. Dr. Miller cleared his throat, "I would recommend perhaps a change of scenery. Some fresh air perhaps. Zere is a good chance zat zis could help his condition."

"So," she started, "what will we do?" Her voice began to break. "I mean, how will we keep our home? What about his work?"

Laura had been compassionate with her husband, to a point. But really. *His extreme feelings of guilt or loss due to Norman's condition.* Bull pucky, she said to herself. Wouldn't it be nice to have the chance to just paint or neglect work because she felt guilty or loss because of Norman? Then, wouldn't they all just be in a fine mess. No. This wouldn't do at all. But she listened to Dr. Miller respectfully as he continued.

Dr. Miller quietly suggested, "I vill speak with ze board at church. A temporary medical leave vill be granted perhaps."

The Bishop did, indeed, grant a leave, and so tearfully Laura began to box up all of their possessions. Piano music played on and off from the study. Henry played melody after melody as Laura packed. She shook her head as, in the background, she could hear the notes of mournful hymns, symbolic of their lives.

She so hated to leave their sweet parsonage. She cried as she placed the bone china teacups back into the cupboard for the final time. She looked around at her freshly painted walls, the darling front porch with the violets she had planted. Violets, she always thought, looked like tiny little monkey faces in blues, yellows, and purples, staring up at her. She walked up the stairs and opened the door to Rose's nursery with the dainty rose bud wallpaper. Her fingers traced the buds. Laura hated to think of another family moving into the house she had so painstakingly made their home.

Flora had gotten Laura some boxes from the local market. She grabbed a large cardboard box that would be a good size to pack Henry's paintings. She went toward the hallway outside of Henry's study. There against the wall, dozens of canvases were stacked.

She grabbed the first painting in the stack and took a long look at the details Henry had created. It was a lovely coastal scene. There were fields of lupine, lavenders and purples and pinks, proudly lining a sandy path toward the rocky Maine coast. The shore was dotted with terns and sandpipers. Frothy waves were crashing against the beach leaving bits and pieces of mussel and clam and scalloped shells in the wake on the sand.

It struck Laura then. As she was nursing the baby, as she was bathing Norman, as she was cleaning the house, as she was cooking the meals, as she was worried sick about Henry...he was here. He was here, in his mind, painting, at this beach. He was able to escape.

Laura calmly brought the painting into the parsonage kitchen. She laid it down against her butcher block. She opened the drawer next to the stove. She grabbed her largest kitchen knife and pierced it through the center of the canvas.

Chapter 24:

Aunt Hildy was the only direct family member of Laura's, in Wilton, who owned a car. Her husband left it to her when he died.   Once she had the car in her possession, she learned to drive, kind of. The family arranged for Aunt Hildy to pick up Henry, Laura, Norman and baby Rose at the parsonage in Livermore and drive the family all back to Ma and Pa's farm on Walker Hill.

Aunt Hildy was Henry's sister.   She was commonly recognized to be as mean as a snake. She had earned that recognition from decades of bad behavior. She careened into the parsonage driveway, where the family waited on the porch for her arrival. Nearly all of the items in the parsonage belonged to the church, so there were only a few meager boxes and bags, that Laura had neatly packed, which needed to be thrown into the boot of Aunt Hildy's car.

Aunt Hildy screeched to a halt and jumped out from behind the steering wheel. She opened the trunk and Henry vacantly picked up the parcels, barely acknowledging his sister. He placed them in the trunk, and Laura began to pick up Norman, now a 60 pound little boy. Hildy looked down at the empty wheelchair sitting on the porch.

"Well what the hell do you think I can do with that thing?" she spat out the words causing Laura to recoil.

"Hildy, dear," Laura said, clearing her throat out of nerves, recovered from the harshness of her sister-in-law's tone, "we will need to take it with us. This *thing* functions as your nephew's legs," Laura said matter of factly. She left no room for argument.

Hildy turned to Henry and pointed at the boxes. "Get those damned boxes back on out of the trunk Henry." He sighed but mechanically obliged her orders. Hildy lifted the chair and placed it in the trunk, and then she positioned the parcels around the wheels. "Well I guess we'll just leave this bastard open," she said indicating the open trunk.

Laura laughed at the vulgar language. What was a girl to do? The unexpected words, so plainly spoken after years of living as "the minister's wife," seemed to almost be a healing balm to her soul. "Yup," she said popping Norman into the back seat. She went to the front porch to grab Rose in her Moses basket. "Let's just leave the bastard open," she repeated and found the words felt good on her tongue.

She jumped into the back seat and placed the basket between herself and Norman. Henry got into the front seat, and Hildy jerked the car into reverse, forcing everyone in the car to jolt forward.

"Hold onto your hats," Hildy shouted, "this car is turning out to be a giant piece of shit." Laura instinctively reached for both Norman and baby Rose, as she was tossed to and fro in the backseat with every jerking move of the car.

And, with that, they headed to a new life on Walker Hill. Livermore was in the rearview mirror.

Chapter 25:

The house atop Walker Hill revealed itself as Aunt Hildy's Oldsmobile crested the hill. Saying it was a sight for Laura's sore eyes would be a dramatic understatement. The entire ride from Livermore was spent holding on for dear life, careening around sharp corners, bouncing, heads to the ceiling, when potholes were slammed into without regard.

The only good thing about the ride was the fact that the experience prompted some rare dialogue and reaction from Henry. He had been a man of few words for the past several months. Hildy hit the brakes unexpectedly, nearly propelling them both through the windshield, as she approached a pothole about the size of Kentucky. "For the love of God Hildy. Slow this machine down at once. You will kill us all."

Hildy was unfazed by the scolding, and ground the car back into gear, swerving and jerking back and forth, her strong hands gripping the wheel. She simply responded loud enough for all to hear, "Ungrateful people get on my last nerve."

Henry quickly retorted, "Had I been told about your driving skills, I would have walked from Livermore." Hildy just snorted at that, but Laura delighted in his remarks. It was the closest thing she had heard that could be considered a joke in months.

Continuing down the road, Hildy probed a bit, "So, what'd you quit your job or get fired?"

Henry didn't answer right away, so Laura chimed in from the back seat, "Henry is just taking a bit of time off to get some fresh air and rest."

"Hummmphhh," snorted Hildy. "Sounds fishy to me," and they jounced on.

Staring straight ahead, Henry quietly but clearly said, "Why don't you just shut up."

Laura, again, saw this response as a sign of hope. At least he was responding.

And then, wonderfully, they turned onto Walker Hill. Home.

Chapter 26:

Ma and Pa said they could hear the Oldsmobile approaching from a mile away. The sound of an engine was pretty unfamiliar up on Walker Hill, so the car might as well have been Orville and Wilbur Wright flying an airplane overhead or a rocket to the moon.

Both Ma and Pa came running down the worn front porch steps, arms outstretched for their grandbabies. Pa fumbled around the car door to get his hands on Norman. He plucked Norman up and out of that seat and clutched his big grandson to his chest. Norman's feet now hung past Pa's pants pockets. He was getting so big.

Ma grabbed baby Rose out of the Moses basket and held her up to the sky, staring into her big brown eyes. "Oh my, oh my, what a fine beauty we have here! What shall we do, what shall we do with such a pretty little thing?" Ma clucked to no one in particular.

Laura gave her father a quick peck on the cheek and then wrapped her arms around Ma. "Here now, here now, my girl," Ma said holding baby Rose in one arm and wrapping the other around her daughter. "Here now, here now." No other words needed to be said.

Hildy wasted no time pulling the wheelchair and the bags out of the boot of her car. She obviously wasn't comfortable around all this show of emotion. She plunked it all down on the ground, and muttered, "I never met such an ungrateful lot in all my years."

Laura attempted to offer her gratitude, but by the time she turned around, she could see it was to no avail.

Hildy slammed the car door with exaggerated angst, and disappeared down over the steep bankings of Walker Hill. They could hear the grinding of the gears and the scraping of brakes for some time, and the dust her car kicked up, lingered in the air in a big billowing cloud.

Chapter 27:

To say the house on Walker Hill was modest would not tell the whole story. The kitchen had open shelving exposing yellow ware bowls interspersed with large wooden bowls Pa had carved from fallen maple trees. He designed them for Ma to use for her dough as she kneaded her bread. He carved different sizes for different breads: daily bread, brown bread, sweet breads and biscuits. A butcher block sat in the center of the kitchen, and was always lightly dusted with the remnants of flour. There was a deep metal farm sink and a pump that pulled ice cold water straight from Wilson Lake into the sink. A tin cup always hung next to the pump handle on a wrought iron hook, making sure a cold drink was always within grasp. Pa had built the entire house with his bare hands.

Ma, although unspoiled and the complete opposite of fancy, had a whimsical side. That particular character trait was evident, particularly in the kitchen. One day, the mailman delivered a book of wallpaper samples from Sears and Roebuck. Ma was delighted with that book, and poured over it, choosing her favorite wallpaper, changing her mind daily about which paper she liked the best. Eventually, reality dictated that she would never be able to afford the wallpaper of her choice, but she couldn't let go of the idea of having a wallpapered kitchen.

On a particularly inspired morning, Ma tore all of the pages of the wallpaper book out of the catalogue, and glued them to the kitchen wall, making a sort of patchwork crazy quilt in an otherwise colorless home. She stood back afterwards and admired her handiwork, and indeed, she had created quite a unique appearance and always got many comments from her few visitors. She always gave her guests the same response when asked about her kitchen, "Well, I couldn't choose which paper I liked best, so I chose them all!" She always got a good laugh out of that!

Laura loved sitting in Ma's kitchen. Hanging from the barn beams were drying herbs; therefore, the kitchen was heavily fragranced, depending on the time of year, with lavender, thyme, sage, spearmint, rosemary, and oregano. There was always a savory stew bubbling from the cast iron pot sitting on the top of the cook stove, and Ma was never, ever too distracted or busy to sit and enjoy a cup of tea.

Ma was completely fascinated with England and the royal family. When she brought a cup of tea to her mouth, she would often say, "There is no difference between me and the Queen Elizabeth in how we enjoy our cup of afternoon tea." This would give her a huge laugh, and she would add, "well, except I had to make this tea myself, and I guess maybe the Queen is having hers served on a silver platter." Then she would hold her pinky finger in the air and say with her mock British accent, "Jolly good tea, isn't it luv?"

As Laura sat with Ma in the patchwork kitchen, she immediately was filled with gratitude. Oh yes, without question she would miss some of the wonderful conveniences of the parsonage she had grown accustomed to. She would miss her hot and cold running tap. She would miss her flushing toilet and her warm bath. She did love her ringer washing machine, but her eyes became misty watching Ma lovingly spoon dollops of her homemade apple butter into Norman's open mouth. She knew then, in that very moment, she would trade all of the modern conveniences known to mankind for the love that was present in the kitchen that day.

Laura jounced baby Rose on her knee, admiring her baby's growing ringlets around her face. She looked outside and saw Henry setting up his easel next to the chicken coop, visibly annoyed and exasperated as he was waving away the noisy feathered flock that was gathering all around his feet.

Chapter 28:

Pa was out there, she was sure. He was either working the soil of one of his fields, or sawing wood for Ma's cook stove. Ma always said Pa was a "dreamer." "That father of yours is a dreamer. Thinks he's on the Broadway stage when he's out there," but she would smile, shaking her head, as she said it.

Pa was out there. He was, in fact, sawing firewood for Ma, thinking about his son and Laura's brother, Roger. Roger had gone missing in the war since last spring. The last they had known, he had been in Germany, but there had been no word other than a simple post card hand delivered to Roger's young wife last spring:

"We regret to inform you your husband has been declared missing in action during a combat mission in Germany."

Those words. That was all. "Declared missing." What was a father to do? He continued to saw his wife's firewood. The woodpile had been getting low.

Back and forth, he pulled the blade. The movement was soothing. It was satisfying when, at last, the log fell at his feet. He bent and tossed it onto the growing pile and placed another log on the sawhorse. Roger, Roger, his mind called for his son. And he sawed and the words of his ancestor came to mind. Pa believed, through years of family lore, that he was a distant relative of Henry Wadsworth Longfellow. This belief gave Pa a sense of pride, as he played Longfellow's words in his head, again and again.

> "...We should find in each man's life,
>
> sorrow and suffering enough
>
> to disarm all hostility."

Pa, carefully placing another log onto the sawhorse, gazed toward the chicken coop and saw his son in law, looking out onto the horizon, paint brush in hand. The words he had just spoken rang true, and Pa thought of the words once again: "...we should find in each man's life sorrow and suffering to disarm all hostility..." He felt his heart soften, as he watched Henry, and went back to sawing wood.

Ma wiped her hands on her apron, and gently cleaned Norman's mouth, swiping up any messiness from his lunch. "There, there Norman. Now wasn't that tasty," she said as she tamped his face with the cloth. Ma placed the dishes in the sink, and she turned to Laura who was nursing Rose. "Look at those two out there would you?" and she shook her head in mock disgust.

Laura rose and looked out onto Walker Hill. Pa was sawing wood, and about 75 yards away from the woodpile Henry stood painting at his easel. "Don't you wonder what they are thinking about," Ma said absently shaking her head and going back to the dishes in sink.

Chapter 29:

*Before a vaccine was introduced in the late **1940s**, pertussis, more commonly known as **whooping cough**, was a leading cause of childhood illness and death in the United States.*

The sound brought Laura bolt upright in her feather ticking bed. Next to her, Henry awakened in equal alarm. There is no sound that can quite mimic the horrific noise from deep within the chest of a child with whooping cough. First Norman, then Rose, both children contracted the dreaded affliction.

The insistent and constant sound of his two children's rattling chests, their hacking and choking and coughing, as horrible as it was, seemed to jolt Henry back from the abyss. Wherever he had been, far away and completely in his own head, he was now present and propelled into action. He had always been there when Norman was having his seizures, and quite wonderfully, he returned to be by Laura's side, for the children's months long bout with whooping cough. There was no option. Laura, as strong as she was, could not have minded them alone.

Ma and Pa. Laura and Henry. All four were constantly rotating shifts to care for Rose and Norman. Each slept in ten or twenty minute catnaps when a moment allowed, but no one had slept solidly through the night in weeks. Both children were tossing in fever soaked sheets, continuously gasping for air. Ma had boiling pots on the stove, trying to keep the air moist for the children's sore throats and fluid filled lungs.

High fevers, deep rattling coughs, and sleepless nights. That had been life on Walker Hill. Henry and Laura would take turns filling the bathtub with cold water, lowering first a quaking toddler, Rose, into the cold tub, and next a shivering ten year old boy, Norman into the tub. They would cool down from their dangerous burning temperatures and delirium to milder fevers, but the illness hung on like a bur to wool.

During the daytime, Ma and Laura would boil bone broth, and bring the nutrient dense briny liquid to the children's mouths, but neither child had any appetite whatsoever. The constant coughing fits left the children weak and nauseous. They just tossed their heads back and forth, fighting the spoon and lost in delirious dreams.

All of the adults were sick with worry, but helpless against the seemingly relentless timeline of this sickness.

Even Aunt Hildy had a soft place in her heart for what was happening with the children atop of Walker Hill. She drove to the house and, surprisingly, delivered some molasses cookies. She stood on the stoop of the front porch, not daring to break the threshold for fear of contracting the illness that permeated the household.

Pa went to the door, Norman in his arms. Hildy stepped back, "My God, you look a fright." Pa had dark circles under his eyes and standing in his t-shirt and suspenders, she could see he had lost weight. The house smelled of Camphor and Mentholatum Rub. She startled and shook her head as she heard the hollow coughing coming from the back bedroom.

"Jumping Jehovah," Hildy said as Henry came into sight, holding a howling, wheezing four year old Rose in his arms. Her lovely little face was crumpled in misery, and her cheeks were flushed with fever. "You all look like the devil," she barked as she thrust her basket forward. "I brought you some cookies. From the wretched looks of you all, you better eat some of them before you lose your britches."

Henry weakly thanked his sister, but she didn't seem comfortable with any kind of emotional exchange. "Well," she sputtered backing up on the stoop, "I hope no one breaks a tooth on them." And she left as quickly as she came.

Pa stood there holding the cookies in one hand and his grandson in the other. He and Henry watched as the Oldsmobile wheels spun out on the gravel road. Hildy couldn't get away fast enough, thinking she could out run the whooping cough. The image struck both men as comical, and they shared a good, if not exhausted, laugh for the first time in ages.

Ma came in, wiping her brow on her apron with bed sheets in her arms, to see what all the ruckus was about. Pa could barely get the story out he was laughing so hard, so Henry described his sister's tires spinning and watching her, "Take off like a bat out of hell."

Ma busted out laughing too. "I don't know why she was in such a hurry," Ma sputtered out, "she's too dang mean to get the whooping cough. Even the whooping cough is scared of that biddy." And they all got in on another round of laughter. The sound of laughter was the perfect tonic for everyone's soul.

Chapter 30:

Once a year, a photographer came to Wilton. He set up his studio in the back of the Sears and Roebuck. Ma came home one afternoon from Merchant's General Store with the Sears and Roebuck flier in hand, advertising the dates the photographer would be in town.

"Laura," Ma said excitedly, "The photographer is going to be here next month, and I just realized, we don't have a single picture of the children." Laura carefully looked over the flier. "I want you to take the children to be photographed," Ma implored with rare enthusiasm.

"Ma," she said, "you know Henry and I can't afford this," and she handed the flier back to her mother. Henry hadn't received a paycheck in nearly four years, and all the money he and Pa made on the farm went right back into the farm and toward the food and provisions the family needed while living there.

Ma went to the pantry and pulled a quart sized Mason jar down from the top shelf. "Oh I keep some spare change in here. I just toss it in here from time to time when I sell a hen or Pa has a good harvest," and she poured a sizeable amount of change out onto the butcher block.

Laura was absolutely flabbergasted. She had no idea Ma would have some money of her own. Laura had never had any money set aside. She had no money of her own, and she really had no idea if Henry had any money. It was such a delightful surprise to discover this delicious little secret about Ma. Laura could have been knocked over with a feather!

"And besides," Ma added with a wink, "I already signed the children up. You need to have them there on May 4 at 10:30. We will gussy these kids up like nobody's business and get a professional photograph of these beauties. I'll have Pa make two big frames for the wall. "

"Well now," Laura said looking down at the flier with a smile, "That is something to truly look forward to."

Ma gathered up the change in her fist and carefully eased the coins back into her jar while watching the window to be sure Pa was nowhere in sight. "Now Laura," she said firmly, "this money jar is to remain a secret between the two of us."

Laura quickly answered, "You can trust me Ma," loving every minute of being in on the conspiracy.

Chapter 31:

May 4 arrived, but there would be no photographs. Everyone held out hope that Norman and little Rose would be healthy enough to travel to town for pictures, but it was not to be.

Laura was so disappointed. She held that date in her head, night after night, and day after day. While she rinsed out and scrubbed Norman's cotton diapers on the washboard, she would say, "this is only temporary, he will be well soon."

As she changed the fever soaked sheets of her children's beds, pinning them to the clothesline, watching them dance against the wind, "this is only temporary, they will be well soon." But the coughing continued, and the fever persisted. Day after day, it was the same. She spoon fed them against their will, while they thrashed their heads to and fro on their pillows. Exhausted and defeated, hearing the gagging and choking coughs that were the monotonous soundtrack for her life, on May 3, she knew for certain, it wasn't to be.

She had pinned the flier, with one of Ma's straight pins, to the crazy quilt kitchen wallpaper as a constant reminder that life would be normal again. The sun would rise. She would spit shine her children, dress them up, fuss with their hair, and they would stroll into town for their 10:30 photograph appointment.

On the morning of the appointment, Ma could see the disappointment in Laura's face. Ma knew how much Laura had been looking forward to her trek into town with the children. "Listen girl," Ma turned to Laura, her face brightening with a new idea, "Why don't you go ahead and take a lovely walk into town and cancel the appointment. It would do you good to get out of here for a bit."

Laura couldn't think of the last time she had been alone anywhere. Then Ma, cheerfully and forcefully (and completely out of character), slipped three dollars into Laura's hand. "And while you are in town, go to the Clip and Curl and get your hair done."

That seemed like an extraordinary indulgence. Money certainly didn't grow on trees and she never once had known Ma to ever have her hair done by a beautician. For Laura's whole life, Ma wore her hair in exactly the same way. Her hair in a tight bun held in the nape of her neck by large pins. Laura started to object, but Ma would not hear of it.

Ma looked Laura directly in the eyes. "Laura. I have watched you tend those babies for almost four years now. You have never once complained. You have never once questioned why? I want you to take a minute and let your mother treat you to something special," Ma's voice started to crack a bit and tears formed in her eyes, which stunned Laura. "You go on now and get dressed, " Ma barked out, hastily wiping her eyes with the edge of her gingham apron with more than slight annoyance, "Pa and Henry and I will watch these children."

That was it then. There was no question. Laura was going to go into town and get her hair done. "Well," she thought, "this is really something special." Her disappointment transformed into an excitement she couldn't remember feeling in some time.

Chapter 32:

It was quite a distance into the village of Wilton. It was nearly a three mile walk, one way. Laura put on her Sunday dress, but wore her every day shoes for the trek, as she knew the way home, the final mile, would be steep and up hill all of the way!

Just having herself to mind was unfamiliar. She barely could catch her breath with the titillating excitement of being alone. Had it been years since she was alone? She had to think. Norman was ten years old. She had never once left him in anyone else's care. It was baffling to think she had not had a shred of time to herself for a decade.

Walking felt so wonderful. She took beautiful long strides. Not having the barrier of a wheelchair or a stroller in front of her felt so freeing. Not being able to quell the enthusiasm she felt at the experience, she began to jog a bit. Was she 29 years old now? My goodness. The days did pass so slowly, she reflected, but the years were so fast.

Her jog became a run. She felt 15 again, back at Walker Hill, as a school girl. Those days she would walk to school every day, with her two older sisters and her brother, Roger. Roger. Where was he now? She pushed the thoughts away. She needn't spoil her few hours of freedom with worry about her brother. There was time for that later.

Down, down, down the hill she ran. Each pounding step announcing she was alone. She was free. She was free. She was free. Faster, faster still she ran, her heart pounding in her chest, tears, not happy, not sad, streaming like a river down her face.

Laura ran until the ground leveled off and Walker Hill was behind her, a veritable mountain in all of its glory. She disgustedly wiped the tears from her face with the backs of her hands. No time for that sort of nonsense today, she scolded herself.

As she approached the little village, she suddenly felt self-conscious. Being up on the farm, Ma didn't indulge vanity. Ma barely, if ever, looked in a mirror as far as Laura knew. Laura realized then, all sweaty and dusty, she must have looked a fright.

As Laura approached the village, she found the familiar old spigot in the town square, steadfast and ready to present her with an icy drink before heading into the tiny beauty shop, The Clip and Curl. The cool drink helped bring her head back around, and she took in a deep breath and smoothed the apron of her dress before entering the hairdresser's.

Mrs. Theriault, with her perfect make up and hair tousled perfectly in an up-do, was thickening a bit around the waist but still glamorous for Wilton, Maine. She was sweeping hair clippings from around her chair when Laura walked in. Laura had gone to grade school with Mrs. Theriault's daughter, Susie, but they hadn't seen one another in years. Mrs. Theriault stopped and placed one hand on her hip, while the other held the broom. "Why Laura Rowe, is that you dear?" she said looking straight into Laura's big brown eyes.

"Yes, yes it is Mrs. Theriault, " Laura said self consciously, "Ma gave me some money to see if maybe I could get my hair done today."

Mrs. Theriault looked delighted, and put her arms around Laura. "Well you have certainly come to the right place. Just wait until I tell Susie. She asks about you all the time," Mrs. Theriault said as she pulled Laura toward her chair. "Oh my goodness. Look at this wonderful thick hair and all of these curls. What my clients wouldn't give for this natural beauty."

Laura had never had her hair shampooed by anyone except Ma before. She could hardly believe how good it felt. She never wanted it to end. The scent of the shampoo and the billowing suds of the fine soap were something she would remember for years to come. Mrs. Theriault chattered and chattered away, but Laura just wanted to be lost in the sensation of the shampoo, the warm water pouring on her head, the massaging of her scalp, and the feeling of being fussed over.

Laura's hair was trimmed and set, and she was placed beneath an electric dryer. When her hair was dry, Mrs. Theriault brushed it out and sprayed it firmly into place, leaving Laura in a cloud of aerosol mist. She then turned Laura around toward the mirror with a grand flourish.

"Voila," Mrs. Theriault said dramatically, and Laura nearly believed she was in Paris. She scarcely recognized herself. She looked as if she were one of the fashion models she had seen in magazines. She just kept staring. How could it be?

Mrs. Theriault could sense how thrilled Laura was with the way her hair had come out, and she, too, was caught up in the moment. It was so lovely to take care of this unspoiled and sweet young woman. Mrs. Theriault had heard about the birth of Norman and, through the news in town, she knew the children had had an awful bout with whooping cough. She was more than happy to do a little extra for her daughter's classmate. "Oh, wait right there Laura," she said as if she had a revelation, "Wait one more minute." She ran into the other room and rummaged in her closet.

When Mrs. Theriault returned, she had a little tube of lipstick. Mrs. Theriault put a bit on the tip of her finger and ran it across Laura's lips. Laura smiled radiantly when she saw her rouge lips. Then Mrs. Theriault rubbed a bit more on each of

Laura's prominent cheekbones. She then stood back and admired her work.

Chapter 33:

Laura left The Clip and Curl thinking the day could not possibly get any better. She gave Mrs. Theriault a quick hug and a peck on the cheek and off she went.

Laura's next stop was the Sears and Roebuck. She felt much more confident walking into the store than she had The Clip and Curl, knowing she had a fine hairdo and a bit of color on her face. She noted the clock said 10:00. She still was in time to properly cancel the studio photograph appointment for her children. She asked the front desk where she could find the photographer, and the clerk pointed her in the right direction. The studio was set up straight in the back of the store, tucked away in a little corner.

Rounding the corner, in the rear of the Sears and Roebuck, Laura's heart sank when she saw a young couple holding their bonneted baby in a christening gown, posing for their photograph. She felt a deep disappointment that she couldn't have her own two beautiful children here, next in line to pose, as had been the original plan.

She saw and heard the tiny explosion of the flash, and then a young man came out from behind the drape, which was placed over the camera. He ambled over to the couple and repositioned them and the baby, expertly tipping the woman's head in one direction, positioning the man's hand just into the opening of his vest. He pulled the baby's bonnet back a tad so it wouldn't cover the lovely baby's sweet pale face. He seemed satisfied that the smart looking trio were in the proper place, and he then disappeared beneath the camera's red velvet cloth. Once again, the pop of the flash sounded, and Laura could smell the sulfur.

Within minutes, the little family had their final picture taken. Laura, who had been waiting there all the while, shyly approached the photographer as he was repositioning his backdrop for his next appointment. "Excuse me sir," she began.

He turned toward her absently, but when he looked up and saw her, she clearly had his full attention. His eyes immediately lit up as he took her in. Who was this beautiful woman, he thought, gazing at her ruby lips, her big brown eyes, her statuesque figure. "How can I help you?" he asked politely, staring directly into her eyes without blinking.

"Sir," she started again, blushing, quite aware of this man's opinion of her appearance, "my children had an appointment to have their photograph taken at 10:30. Their names are Norman and Rose Brooks and my mother made this appointment weeks ago, but I'm afraid they aren't able to be here," her voice quavered as she finished. "They are quite ill," she stammered, "with whooping cough."

He could immediately sense how disappointed she was. "What a shame," he said, and he meant it. Traveling town to town, he had heard of dozens of severe outbreaks of whooping cough all over New England.

"Well, yes. Yes it is," Laura answered, noting that he had not taken his gaze away from her. "I just came here to be sure you knew," she finished. "We don't have a telephone, so I walked here so you wouldn't be held up waiting for us," and she turned to leave. "I'm terribly sorry for any inconvenience we may have caused," she uttered as she backed through the doorway.

"Did you say, you walked?" he repeated. "I hope it wasn't too far."

"Oh yes, I did walk, but it was no problem," and she meant every single word, remembering her run down from the hill. "It was actually very lovely to walk here today," she said in all sincerity.

"Well it would be a shame to waste your time," and then he had an idea, and he raised an eyebrow, quite pleased with himself. "Why don't I take your photo?"

Laura turned back toward him and laughed out loud dismissing the thought. Then, she could see from his expression that he truly meant it. She remembered her reflection from The Clip and Curl. Laura reached up and touched her hair ever so slightly, making sure it hadn't been a dream. "My photo?" she repeated.

"Yes, yes, I would love to take your photograph," and he took her hand and pulled her toward the stool positioned in the front of his backdrop. Laura obliged, hesitantly, very aware of the fact that her hand was in his. She sat, embarrassed, on the stool, smiling nervously.

"I...I don't know," she stammered, "it was for the children. My mother gave it to me as a gift," she said, guiltily thinking of the jar of coins, saved so sacredly by her mother, held for special purposes.

"Oh no, no, you misunderstand," he interjected quickly, "This will cost you nothing. I *want* to take your photograph. For no cost at all." And then he added looking straight into Laura's eyes, "Ma'am, if you don't mind my saying, you are quite a rare beauty."

"Oh," Laura blushed deeply, realizing how very much she was enjoying his compliment. Ma would be so upset thinking how this talk was going straight to Laura's head. Ma would always say, "Pretty is as pretty does." She didn't ferret out compliments too often. She never had. "It's what's inside that matters Laura," she would say whenever Laura was hinting for praise regarding her appearance. She could scarcely think of a single time when Ma or Pa had ever called her pretty.

Laura looked down, and saw her chapped hands. Oh, life was so hard on her hands, she thought. Her hands were always in tubs of cold water, using the harsh lye bars of soap, scouring rags on the washboard, applying gobs of mentholatum rub, giving the children their baths, scrubbing the diapers, hanging the sheets in the cold air, and carrying fire wood. Her hands were the hands of a hard laborer, she thought. She put one self-consciously over the other trying to hide her cracked and chapped fingers.

The photographer backed away to take her fully into his view. He seemed to notice something out of place, and crouching, moved toward her like a tiger to his prey. Her heart quickened, as his hand came up and took a small pin curl of hair, and very carefully, tucked it neatly behind her ear. The touch felt so intimate. Did he notice the heat in her face? She noticed the softness of his hands, so unlike her own.

He backed away once again, and nodded his head with a satisfied grin, pleased with her pose. "Okay," he directed, "look over here...past my shoulder," and he ducked himself beneath the shawl on his camera. Laura held her pose, and her breath, until she heard the pop of the flash.

Once she heard the flash, she couldn't help but burst into laughter and she immediately relaxed her position, "My gracious," she exclaimed, "that certainly was awkward." He smiled, delighted at her reaction.

"Well," he responded without hesitation, "it may have felt awkward, but you are a natural Miss…" and he did hesitate this time, not knowing her name.

"Missus," corrected Laura, "Brooks, but you can call me Laura."

The photographer approached Laura then with his gentleman's hand extended, "Pleased to meet you Laura," and he gripped her hand. "My name is Matthew. Matthew Hanes."

Laura hadn't expected this kind of attention, and she certainly was not sure what to do about it, but she found she was enjoying it. She noticed Matthew was a very handsome man. She wasn't certain what his age was…maybe the same as her own, but he was tall and handsome, and sure of himself. "Laura," he continued, "would you indulge me and allow me to take one more photo?"

"Oh, I don't know," she started.

Quickly Matthew pleaded, "Just one, looking off the other way. One more photograph capturing your lovely profile. There is something quite beautiful in your face, a depth, something…" he was searching for words. "Just one, Laura," he implored, staring directly at her. "I will make it fast."

"Well, I don't see the harm I suppose," she said, and he quickly came toward her, repositioning her against the backdrop, lightly placing his hand beneath her chin to lift her face an inch.

She could scarcely breathe with his touch.

Chapter 34:

Although she had run as fast as she could into town, heading back to Walker Hill, she walked. And she walked slowly, dragging her feet, scuffing up sand and dust all along her way.

Was it something of a dream she had just experienced? First, she had the joyful freedom of the walk to town. Then, she got to go to The Clip and Curl for that lovely shampoo and style. And then the photograph and….well, she met Matthew. For however Matthew had made her feel, she wasn't quite ready to let go of that feeling just yet. Laura walked as slowly as she could because she truly could not bear the thought of this day coming to an end.

Matthew told her, very specifically, that the photographs he had taken would be developed and ready in exactly seven days. He asked if she would come back in a week to pick them up. "Well, we shall see," Laura said without commitment. It had been years since she had been alone, let alone in town. How could she imagine coming back again in only one week?

Step by step, Laura made her way home to Walker Hill. As she crested the hill, she could see Pa and Henry, working on the woodpile side by side. Both were quiet men. The two of them recently seemed to have forged a bond, and although few words were ever exchanged, they appeared to find a certain comfort in one another's presence.

Henry had not mentioned returning to the ministry for years. Although Laura didn't believe any formal agreements had ever been decided upon, he and Pa seemed to have a silent arrangement and understanding of their roles on the farm. Most days, they both worked in silence. Ma said they were wrangling with their demons. It probably was true.

Every day Pa spent some time looking out over the hills, thinking about Roger, most likely. Where was his boy? In some field in Germany, in some forested glen, a prisoner of war? Dead? Alive? Wounded? Oh how it tortured his soul. Where was his only son?

Pa couldn't bear to think of his boy in pain, so he would imagine all different scenarios...that Roger was in an abandoned farmhouse with plenty of food to live off the land, or that he was being hidden by a kind family, fed and clothed and safe, until the war ended. He filled his mind with any possibility that left his son alive and without suffering of any sort.

Henry wondered where his boy was too. Although Norman sat right in front of him, his wheelchair parked, his face leaning toward the sun; it was not the boy he had imagined. He had no words. He had no joy. If he did know happiness, he had no vehicle to express it. He just was. And Henry felt forsaken by God; he felt somehow that God had broken a promise to him. Afterall, Henry had given his life to serve and yet, still, He gave him a son that felt like a deal gone wrong. Where was the boy he had prepared for?

So both men wrangled with their demons. A log needing to be cut sat between them both, and as they sawed back and forth, back and forth, both were searching for their sons, and questioning a God they had spent their lives worshipping.

Ma didn't spare her words. She said the two of them were fools. She said, "Well there's no time for wondering why? I don't have a minute to stare off into no man's land. Not while there's work that needs to be done," and she would busy herself in the kitchen. She would grind up Norman's meals, give her simmering pot a stir, rinse her dishes, and boil the diapers. Sometimes Laura would catch her dabbing her eyes with the corner of her apron, or on some days she would just let the tears run down her cheeks, but she never gave in to it. Laura never mentioned her mother's tears and her mother never offered why they were there. She didn't have to.

Laura asked her one day, "Ma, how do you keep going?"

Her answer was curt, "Well if I stop Laura, I'm pretty sure I won't start up again."

And that was that.

Chapter 35:

Laura understood what her mother meant, "...if I stop, I'm pretty sure I won't start up again." She hadn't had time to herself for years, but since the day she returned from her fleeting moments in town, she felt different somehow. Really different. She felt changed in a way she could not explain, and she couldn't seem to hide the new discontentedness and restlessness she was feeling at her core.

Although the children's coughing was slowing, and their sleep was more settled, and they had even begun to regain their appetites, she felt suffocated anyhow. Smothered. Before, as she changed Norman's soiled diapers, then scoured them, and boiled them, she just did it without a second thought. Now, she did it with disdain, resentment. The tasks she hadn't before questioned, now made her angry and she didn't want to do it any more.

She snapped her answers back to Henry when he asked her a question, and he would visibly recoil. She scowled as she boiled the water for doing the evening dishes. She sighed as she brought Rose out to the privy in the cold evening.

Ma noticed. Pa noticed.

Laura watched Pa and Henry outside, and she felt jealous, like a caged animal. She was always inside cooking. Always inside cleaning. Inside tending the children. Every day was the same. She felt joyless and surly.

As she was hanging out the cotton diapers, clipping them to the line with her perennially chapped and sore fingers, Laura thought about the photograph she had taken. She remembered the touch of Matthew's soft fingers on her cheek, lifting her chin. She remembered how beautiful she had felt. She felt a heat she had long since forgotten. Back up on Walker Hill, she couldn't even remember the last time she had seen her reflection in a mirror.

Ma, uncharacteristically, came outside to join Laura one afternoon as she was standing outside with the day's mound of laundry waiting in the basket. She resented the interruption to her daydream. Ma didn't care and she did not waste words, "What's gotten into you Laura? For God's sake girl, you remind me of Aunt Hildy with your crab apple disposition."

Laura looked at her mother, and didn't feel like defending herself. Ma was right. She was crabby. She came forward and admitted how she was feeling to her mother, "Ma, I know. I know I'm terribly grouchy, but Ma," she paused and added with conviction, carefully choosing her words, "I'm just not happy."

Her mother took in what Laura said, and nodded with an exhausted sigh. She moved a step closer to her daughter, and tersely gave her response. "Laura. Why don't you go ahead and show me in the Bible where it says that you are supposed to be happy?"

Laura thought for a moment, and her mother quickly added, "Don't waste your time thinking about that, because let me tell you. It is not there. God doesn't prioritize your happiness, and so neither should you."

And with that, Ma abruptly turned on her heels and returned to the house to get ready for dinner.

Chapter 36:

The tension rose from her chest constricting her breathing. Her nerves had become a rope, tightening their coiled fibers around her neck. She lurched forward, gasping, dropping Norman's spoon into the metal sink with a percussive clang as she made her way through the kitchen.

She grabbed desperately at her red gingham apron, pulling its ties urgently away from her neck, and tugging it away from her waist. It was choking her. She couldn't breathe. She lunged at the screen door, dropped the apron to the ground, shoving the door open in desperation for the air to fill her lungs. She ran down the weather beaten front steps, bending at the waist, heart pounding, swallowing giant gulps of blessed fresh air that tasted of earth.

Running her hands through masses of unruly mahogany curls, forehead damp with sweat, she slowly stood and steadied her breathing. Calm down now, Laura, for the love of God was the mantra, repeating, inside of her head. Calm down. Calm down. Calm down.

Looking out from tamped down grasses that formed the walkway of her childhood home, out at the view from Walker Hill, she was reminded that the world was not so small. Just her world was small. Her world was microscopic in dimensions, suffocating and narrow.

The field grasses caught her attention. When the wind blew just right, it was as if all of the grasses were dancing. First all the long blades would sway to the right, emerald greens, tans and browns, and pale greens and forest greens. The fronds would stand straight up, pause, and then bow to the front, and then dip, over and over. The symphonic whoosh and whirs of the blades were mesmerizing. Strands of her hair blew from behind her ear, tangling tendrils around her face. Walker Hill. For a place in time, her whole life existed on this one unforgiving slope of landscape.

Could a place be both heaven and hell?

Red breasted robins, cedar waxwings, tiny chickadees, sparrows and wrens, giant black crows, red winged blackbirds, and the occasional whirring humming birds. Dipping up and down, in and out of the grasses. Chirps and warbles, tweets and caws. The melodic sounds of childhood. In and out, up and down, they bobbed through the grasses. The frenetic, cheerful, particular movement of the birds stood boldly in stark contrast of the anguish and monotony being lived out just beyond, inside of the house, on the knoll.

In the background, always in the full bloom of spring, the shrill constant trill of the crickets. The buzzing vibration of giant lazy bumblebees...fat and drunk on the nectar of wildflowers lumbering along, visiting blossom after blossom....the white bloom of lilies of the valley, the proud yellow faces of daisies, the pink and white purple spikes of lupine dotting the horizon, the delicate and intricate lacy patterns of Queen Anne's lace. There was never a shortage of sweet nectar sips on Walker Hill.

Ma and Pa's listing and leaning barn seemed to balance on top of the swell of the hill. Rickety wooden steps led to a smile of a front porch. Ma and Pa had hand-caned rocking chairs positioned with a wooden barrel between them, upside down for a table, to snip beans or shell peas in a bowl they shared. The front door held the only coat of paint on the house. Yellow...once cheerful and bright, now a, pale hue reminding all who entered of the optimism of yesteryears, like a dimming light.

Outside the clothesline almost always held sheets or towels or billowing shirts, flapping about wildly, fighting the wooden pegs which fastened them to the line against their will.

Winded and worn out after walking the steep path to the house, the barn boards of home reached out to the weary traveler, a welcome sight, no matter how tattered the shutters, regardless how chipped the paint. The path to the yellow door was a warm embrace.

Squinting out to the horizon, the tones of the earth soothed her, calmed her. Slowed her breathing. Somewhere in the distance, in the fields of lupine, she knew Pa stood, looking out at the great beyond, his eyes seeking answers in the distance. Henry

Wadsworth Longfellow was a distant relative. He took great pride in that fact, and he often recited the words of his kin effortlessly into the abyss, arms flailing, audience only in his mind:

> Tell me not, in mournful numbers,
>
> Life is but an empty dream!
>
> For the soul is dead that slumbers,
>
> And things are not what they seem.

His voice steady and strong trailing over and through the dancing weeds and blossoms.

She inhaled, deeply at the waist, one more time before turning toward the house. Inside, she could hear the deep wracking coughs pulling her toward the yellow door...while simultaneously pushing her away from the yellow door. Go in. Go in. Tend them.

Ma's voice broke through the sounds of the cough, "Laura. Laura. Where the devil are you?" Laura sighed and picked up the apron she had thrown to the ground. She pulled the gingham ties to the back of her neck and formed a bow. She could feel the familiar tightening around her throat as she thrust open the screen door.

Chapter 37:

It was very different from the day Ma handed Laura money and practically forced her to go to The Clip and Curl. This time, Ma didn't want Laura to go into town. And she made no bones about it.

"I don't know why you're headed back there. You've got the kids to tend." Ma was scowling, making her case by holding up a broom and dustpan, "I have a lot to do without watching your children too, Laura," Ma chided with more than a hint of suspicion in her voice.

Laura was undeterred. "Henry can watch the kids Ma."

Ma snorted, and Laura quickly answered back, "They are his kids too. He can take a break from helping Pa for one morning." Laura was determined to go into town.

Laura found herself more and more jealous as she watched Pa and Henry outside, hoeing the fields or sawing wood, patching a fence, or nailing shingles to the barn roof. It must have felt so good, that hard heavy work. Their work was man and machine or man against nature. Putting hammer to nail...the pounding...the movement, it must have been a wonderful release.

Laura's work was all human to human interaction. It was all touch and unrelenting human contact. When her work was done right, it involved human tenderness. Changing Norman required Laura to pick him up, pull down his britches, wipe his bottom, powder him, put ointment on him, carefully pin back his diaper, pull on his pants, lift him to his chair, and buckle him in. And this was done multiple times each day to avoid horrible sores that resulted in weeks of treatment.

She couldn't be so cold as not to coo to him, smile down at him, hug him or kiss him on his way back to his wheelchair. He wasn't a robot and neither was she. Her body, his body, both morphed into one until Laura could not tell one from the other. She cleaned and touched and fed his body every bit as often, or maybe more than, her own.

And then, there was her daughter. Rose needed her too. She sometimes felt like she had precious little left to offer her youngest child at the end of the day. Norman required so much tending. In the throes of whooping cough, she pulled Rose to her lap and rocked her deep into the night, trying to keep her upright, easing her choking cough. It occurred to her then, she had not held her baby girl much recently. The weight of her daughter felt unfamiliar compared to the weight of Norman. Rose snuggled up against her mother, feverish and shaking, craving comfort. Laura found herself, once again, craving just the opposite. All she wanted was solitude.

By the time Laura fell into bed beside her husband at night, she had no desire for any more contact. She just wanted sleep.

She could not recall the last time they had been intimate as husband and wife, and she didn't care. She didn't want to touch and she didn't want to be touched by the time she lowered herself into bed at night. If, by some twist or turn in the night, Laura's body happened to brush against Henry's, she would pull herself back and recoil to her own side of the mattress.

But then, she remembered Matthew's touch.

Meanwhile, Ma threw her hands up in disgust. "I don't know why you had your picture taken anyway. Honestly Laura," and she turned back around and headed into the kitchen sputtering loud enough for Laura to hear, "Vanity is the work of the devil."

Laura hollered over her shoulder, "It was free Ma. I don't see the big deal about it," and she closed the yellow door, walked down the front steps, and headed down over the hill.

Laura, once again, breathed giant gulps of air into her lungs. She longed again for the taste of freedom, but this time it tasted different to Laura. Rather than the unfettered flavors of the sweetness of solitude, this time she was choking on, what was it, guilt?

As she walked toward town, she imagined seeing Matthew again. She remembered again with shame, how it felt when his soft fingers pushed her pin curl into place, and she recalled the heat she experienced when he gently lifted her chin for the second photo.

She walked on toward town trying to enjoy the feeling of being alone. She tried to push away Ma's comments about vanity. She wished she could shed the image of Ma's disapproving face.

Chapter 38:

When Laura was about a mile from reaching town, an Oldsmobile came screeching up behind her, nearly scaring her to death. Laura startled as she heard the brakes grind to a halt. Aunt Hildy blared on the horn, as if she hadn't already been noticed.

"Hey there Missy. Looks like someone could use a lift," Hildy hollered out the window to Laura.

Laura was a little more than disappointed by the offer. Aunt Hildy had no idea how glorious it was to have a chance to walk in the sunshine, alone and away from home. But, as usual, Hildy was relentless when Laura told her she would just as soon walk. "For God's sake girl. It's another mile to town. Get your little fanny in here and let me give you a ride," Hildy barked out.

Laura gave in. What was she to say at the kind offer?

"So, where you headed Laura Jean?" Aunt Hildy asked.

"Well, I am actually headed to Sears and Roebuck to pick up a photograph I had taken," Laura answered cautiously. It was then that she realized she did not want Aunt Hildy to be any part of the process. It was quite enough to have Ma mad at her. She didn't need Aunt Hildy's two cents thrown in. She held her breath hoping Hildy would not probe any further, but of course that was way too much to ask. Could nothing be sacred for Laura's and hers alone?

"A photograph? Who the heck had a photograph taken from up on Walker Hill?"

Laura then explained her trek into town to cancel the photograph of the children who still suffered from whooping cough, and then she explained the kind offer of the photographer to take Laura's picture instead. "So," Laura finished up, "I am on the way to pick up the photograph that he took of me."

"Hmmmph," Aunt Hildy said after taking it in, and she added, "well, that's weird."

Laura just shrugged.

Chapter 39:

In the car with Aunt Hildy, Laura began to feel self-conscious again. She looked

down at her folded hands, and saw, once again, how chapped and raw they were.

Her hair was no longer as fashionably styled as it had been the day Matthew had

first seen her. Then, it had been clipped back and expertly sprayed and held in

place. Now tendrils spilled out, all around her face, and it was mussed from her walk

down the hill.

Somehow, she convinced Aunt Hildy not to wait for her at the Sears and Roebuck,

and took a deep breath of relief as she got out of the car, thanking Aunt Hildy for the

ride. Laura hopped out of the car, and smoothed the skirts of her dress.

Just as she turned to go into the building, she caught the image of Matthew out of the

corner of her eye, standing and smoking a cigarette in the alley just beyond. He was

such a striking figure. There was no mistaking the fact that her body physically

reacted when she saw him. Laura was certain she felt her heart skip a beat.

Matthew hollered in Laura's direction right away, "Well, there you are," he said as a

wide smile spread across his face. "It's Laura, right?" She could feel the deep heat

of her blushing cheeks, as she walked over to him.

"Hello again, Matthew," she said as she approached him. She had nearly forgotten how handsome he was. His cheekbones were as chiseled as Clark Gable's. His hair was combed back neatly. He had one hand in his pocket, the other held a cigarette and he was bent at the waist, resting one knee on the stoop. He looked like he could have been posed there for one of his own photographs.

"Wait until you see the picture I took of you Missy," he said with a gleam in his eye. "I have thoughts of sending it straight on to Hollywood," he said with a sideways grin, "I believe it would make you a big, big star."

Matthew snuffed out the amber tip of his cigarette on the stoop, and told Laura to follow him. Inside of the studio, he went to a tray and he carefully pulled out her portrait. The portrait was protected by a thin film of parchment paper. Matthew pulled the paper back gently, slowly revealing Laura's face.

Laura was startled when she saw the portrait staring back at her. It was not her beauty that she noticed. Instead, it was her sadness. Her dark eyes looked into the distance, but what was she seeing?

Matthew waited for Laura's response, but there was only silence. When he could wait no longer for her reaction, he asked, "Isn't it beautiful? Do you like it as much as I do?"

Laura continued staring at it, "I look so sad," she quietly whispered. And then her eyes met his.

He looked intently at the portrait trying to see what she was seeing, and then looked back at Laura, "Are you sad?" he asked earnestly.

"I guess I am," Laura said, her eyes brimming with tears, only then realizing the very real sorrow she had been harboring. "I guess I am."

And then, as clear as day, she heard Ma's voice in her head, "Show me where it says in the Bible that you should be happy."

Chapter 40:

Laura wasn't sure what happened in the moments after she had confessed her sadness. Had Matthew considered that an invitation? Had it been an invitation? The moment lived in Laura's mind as a confusing blur of events.

As Laura went to wipe a tear from her eye, Matthew moved in close to her. He reached toward her and wiped the tear with his thumb, brushing his thumb across her cheekbone. It was then that he leaned in to kiss Laura. Feeling his lips against hers was not a complete surprise, nor was it an unpleasant one. She let them linger there for a moment, closing her eyes and savoring the sensation.

Was it a sound that startled her? A door closing? The cash register ringing from the other room? Something jolted her, and she jumped backwards, flustered. Ashamed. What was she doing? A married woman. A mother.

"I'm sorry," Matthew began. "It's just you are so beautiful. I have been thinking about you night and day, Laura, for the past week. Night and day."

Laura interrupted him then. "You know nothing about me. I should not have come back here," and she backed out of the room, "I don't know what I was thinking," she stammered as she left.

Matthew stood crestfallen. He went to offer another apology, but Laura waved him away.

"I shouldn't have come," she continued, imagining Ma's disappointment. Her disapproval. She imagined the twinkle in Ma's eyes when she first counted out the change for the children's portrait.

She still clutched the photograph in her hand, as she ran through the front door of Sears and Roebuck, nearly running into an elderly couple entering the store. She clumsily apologized and then ran to the street.

Chapter 41:

Matthew pushed past the couple in the doorway, and found Laura, standing,

flustered on the sidewalk. He stammered out an apology. Laura's eyes were

brimming with tears and her cheeks were hot with shame.

Laura followed Matthew blindly, as he pulled her along by her hand. "Let's just talk

a moment," he implored as he guided her away from the building. They stopped

after a few steps, next to a red pickup truck that had the name of Matthew's

photography studio painted on the driver side door in black lettering. Matthew

continued his apology as he opened the passenger door for Laura to get in.

Laura got in, but all the while, she was saying, "I should really just go," and then, "I

made a terrible mistake."

Matthew started up the truck while Laura looked around to see if anyone from town

may have noticed that she was getting into a perfect stranger's vehicle. She

recognized no one, and that provided some degree of relief.   As they rumbled down

the road, Laura turned to Matthew, "Where are we going?"

Matthew answered, "Let's just find ourselves a quiet spot to chat," and he looked

from side to side, searching for a spot away from the main road with some privacy.

"You don't know of a spot like that, do you?" he asked, his question filled with more than just the obvious inquiry.

It was in that split second that Laura felt the gravitational pull of a defining moment sitting in front of her. She answered slowly, "I do know of a place," and Matthew smiled as a result.

Laura pointed out a turn that would lead to a woodlot she had visited with Pa as a child. She didn't know to whom it belonged, but she remembered coming here with Pa as he labored day after day with his cousin, cutting in this lot to earn extra money years ago. It was just off the main road, and the truck easily pulled in behind the blind of a cluster of cedar boughs.

Once parked, there was hardly any talking. Was it Laura or was it Matthew who first moved toward the other? It was hard to say. Matthew and Laura quickly became a hot and twisted tangle of passion. Matthew's hands reached hungrily for Laura, and she lost herself in every sensation she allowed herself to feel.

Laura felt like she was somehow hovering over the scene unfolding inside the cab of the truck. Although each touch and each kiss and each sensation deep inside of her was felt, Laura felt as if her mind was detached from all that was happening to her body. And she let it all happen, and she drank in every heated moment as if she had been dying of thirst. She had almost forgotten what it felt like to be a woman. She knew she would wish she had never awakened the memories, because no good would come of it. But for the moment, this one moment in time, she closed her eyes and savored the stolen pleasures her body had been starving for.

Flushed and dazed, Matthew dropped Laura off at the bottom of Walker Hill. No words were exchanged and no future plans were spoken of. She grabbed her photograph and smoothed her skirts before beginning her journey up the steep incline. She could still feel the heat of Matthew's kiss on her mouth. She put her fingers to her lips, holding it there.

Like Ma's jar of money, she also was holding onto a secret she knew she would never reveal.

Chapter 42:

Ma had been true to her word. She didn't take the time to watch the children in Laura's absence. When Laura crested the hill completely out of breath and still feeling flustered, she could see Ma out on the front porch, snipping green beans into a basket. Her mouth was a firm line of displeasure. Pa was nowhere in sight.

Little Rose was gaining strength and putting on weight each day, but still, she remained a tiny, scrawny little mite. She was running around the chicken coop flapping her arms, scaring up the farm fowl. The hens and chickens were clucking like mad, and a delighted Rose, chased them in circles, squealing with joy. Her occasional cough stopped her for a moment, but then she would recover and go after the chickens again. The whooping cough was slowly becoming just a bad memory.

Just beyond the chicken coop, near the well, Henry sat on a plaid, woolen blanket with Norman. Henry was playing a lively song on his harmonica, and Norman sat propped against his father in the sunlight. The sight of the two of them caught Laura's breath. They were such a handsome pair. Why had she not seen it before? The two of them looked so much alike.

Rose saw her Momma coming up the hill, so she gave the chickens a brief reprieve and ran toward Laura, abandoning the flock. Arms outstretched for her mother, Rose ran full steam down the slope. Laura scooped her up, and hugged her deeply.

The children were not accustomed to their mother ever being away from them, so a homecoming welcome was a rare event. With her little girl's arms wrapped around her, Laura squeezed the tears back, feeling a lump in her throat.

Laura walked toward Norman and Henry, Rose in her arms, and her photograph clutched firmly in her hand. Henry looked up and pulled the harmonica away from his mouth. He, too, looked happy to see her. He seemed to be studying her face to see what it was that she was feeling.

She and Rose sat down on the blanket, and Henry held his hand out for the photograph. A man of few words, he peeled back the parchment paper, and he made a low whistling sound, and smiling sideways at her, he said slowly, "Zowie Laura. You look like the spitting image of Rita Hayworth."

Laura leaned back and closed her eyes. The sun felt so good on her face. She heard the compliment, and savored it.

The memory of Matthew's kiss burned in her mind like a stranger harbored there. In all of her life, she had never had a secret.

Chapter 43:

Laura was in the back bedroom replacing the chamber pot where it belonged underneath little Rose's straw mattress. Norman sat in a ray of sunshine, in his wheelchair near the window, dressed and fed and ready for a new day on Walker Hill. Laura could hear Rose out by the hen house, stirring up the poor chickens again, laughing her head off, as was her morning routine.

Pa and Henry must have been out in the fields planting, when Laura heard the sound of a motor outside. Well, that was unusual on the farm, as they rarely had company. They didn't even have mail delivery. Either Pa or Henry had to make the trek down the mile long hill each day if they wanted to fetch the mail.

Curious, Laura peered out of the window, only to see Roger's wife, Kate step out of the car. Laura wasn't certain who was driving, not that it made any difference.

Time stood still for a moment, and then things came into focus as if in a movie reel. Little Rose stopped at the sound of the car pulling up, and Ma must have heard the car too, for she dropped the bucket of milk she had been carrying from the cow barn. Laura watched the milk pour onto the ground into a puddle, but Ma just kept moving forward toward Kate. Ma had pulled her apron up toward her mouth, twisted in a knot in her fist.

Kate reached for Ma, and it was then Laura knew.

Roger was dead.

The primal sound released from Ma was unlike any sound Laura had ever heard on Walker Hill or anywhere, and it brought Pa running from the fields.

Ma dropped to her knees and Kate let her go. Out of the corner of her eye, Laura noticed little Rose running toward her grandmother. Was it instinct that she knew? She ran without hesitation and stood patting her Granny on the back, looking around for another grown up to help. Her little mouth kept whispering, "There there, there, there," patting, patting her Granny's back all the while.

Laura, paralyzed by the scene unfolding before her, came to her senses as she saw Pa run to Ma. He pulled her up to her feet, and they held each other, swaying back and forth, as Henry crested the hill and grabbed Rose, leaving his in-laws to comfort one another.

It occurred to Laura, until that moment, she could not remember a time when she saw her parents in one another's arms. She had never seen them hug, or kiss, or hold hands. But in that moment, with the keening sound of Ma's mournful cries carrying over the entire vast landscape of Walker Hill, through the fields, above the trees, into the valley beyond, she saw what true love looks like.

Henry appeared, breathless and pale in the doorway of the back bedroom, holding Rose in his arms. He moved toward Laura, ready to tell her of her brother's death, but she stopped him. "I know Henry," she said hoarsely, her voice barely audible, and she glanced back outside to her parents, still clinging to one another. "I know."

Henry moved toward his wife, placing one hand on her shoulder. She sensed he was trying to provide her some comfort, but he needn't have bothered. She had lost her brother. She moved away from his hand, and instinctively moved toward Norman. She pushed his chair toward the front door, toward Ma, toward Pa.

Ma's wailing was more than she could stand. Leaving Norman in his chair, and leaving Henry and Rose standing behind, she rushed toward her mother and father, into the unconditional fold of their love.

Somehow, without looking up, Pa knew his girl was standing there. Without releasing Ma, he pulled Laura into the crook of his arm and into their intimate embrace. Ma, Pa and Laura stood there, a tight circle, swooning from the kind of sorrow only "those who have been there" recognize...a painful, crippling, frightening, blinding grief.

For the first time in recent memory, Henry, holding Rose, and with one hand on the back of Norman's wheelchair, did what came naturally. He prayed: *"God, grant me great patience, to wait with courage, as you strengthen my heart..."*

After an indeterminate amount of time, as the sun stood high in the sky, Ma began to pull away from Pa's hold, and turned her head toward the comfort she was receiving from God's word. Henry continued to pray, as little Rose, still in his arms, held her head bowed and her little hands folded in prayer.

Ma reached for her granddaughter and held Rose, and she joined Henry in prayer, first quietly, and then raising her voice to the heavens:

The Lord is my shepherd,

I shall not want.

He maketh me to lie down in green pastures.

He leadeth me beside the still waters

He restoreth my soul...

Henry continued praying, and Laura released her grasp on Pa, watching now as Henry, holding fast to Norman, led his mother into the warm, familiar comfort of the Lord's word. Little Rose still remained bowed in prayer, as Ma raised her voice to the sky:

Yea, though I walk through the valley of the shadow of death

I will fear no evil, for thou art with me,

Thy rod and they staff, they comfort me.

Tears continued to roll down the faces of Ma and Pa, and Kate came over and joined their circle of prayer, sidling up beside the mystified Laura, and grabbing her hand. Voices, joined together, on the magnificent crest of Walker Hill, they all, without thought or preparation, led only by instinct, following Henry's lead:

Thou preparest a table before me in the presence of mine enemies

Though anointest my head with oil

My cup runneth over.

Standing in a circle with her family, with a grief as deep as the soul can feel, Laura's cup truly did "runneth over."

Surely goodness and mercy shall follow me

All the days of my life

And I will dwell in the home of the Lord forever.

Chapter 44:

Roger's body was flown to Maine several weeks after Kate arrived with the devastating news of his death. Knowing Roger would want his final resting place to be Walker Hill, a simple ceremony was planned to "bring Roger home."

Henry and Pa wordlessly got up on that fateful Saturday morning in August, and dug a grave out behind the house. They placed the gravesite beside the massive maple tree where Roger grew up, taking turns on the wooden bench swing, with his three younger sisters.

Kate, Roger's widow, and Laura's two older sisters all remained inside the kitchen carefully following all of Ma's quiet directives. Ruth, the oldest of the girls, was a wonder in the kitchen, and she stood at the helm, baking delicious breads and sweets, quietly assuming the role she knew she was best at. She had a beautiful little three year old girl, Jannie. As Ruth cooked, Jan was tended to outside by her older cousins who loved to watch over this angelic and lovely child.

Helen, the middle daughter, and missionary for Christianity, had been away for years, and hadn't ever gotten the chance to meet Norman. She sat with him and gently held his hand while telling him stories of the wonderful adventures she had been on when she had traveled around the world. Norman quietly rocked back and forth to the sound of her lilting voice. Helen's gentle tones provided a wonderful backdrop for everyone's frayed nerves.

Kate and Roger had two little girls, one older and one younger than Rose. The girls had been accustomed to their father being away in the war for so many years, therefore, they weren't entirely aware of the gravity of the situation. So, the cousins were having a grand time together, in spite of the tragedy at hand. Laura shooed all of them outside to play, to keep the peace, as much as possible, for Ma.

It was roasting hot inside of the Walker Hill kitchen. With only a woodstove for cooking, and all of the anticipated company to feed, Ma scurried around the kitchen wiping her brow. She helped Ruth keep track of the time on the baked goods in the oven so they would be pulled out just as they turned a perfect, golden brown. Ma rubbed several freshly slaughtered chickens with lard, sage and rosemary, and roasted them alongside of the sweetbreads.

Everyone remained busy and focused. There was much to do before 2:00 p.m. when Roger's graveside service would begin. With no time for idle hands, there was no chance for anyone to think about the pine box, draped with an American Flag, in the front room. No one mentioned it, and no one, no matter how hot, left the kitchen for a reprieve into the front room.

Laura stood out in the gardens with a basket on her arm, and a straw hat on her head, in an attempt to remain cool in the blazing hot sun. She was charged with gathering the pole beans and sweet peas. The delicious smells of the baking taking place in the tiny, sweltering kitchen wafted out from behind the front door into the neat rows of the garden plants in which Laura stood.

Laura breathed the scents in deeply, the smells of home, the fragrance of family. In the background, Laura could hear the steady sound of the spades digging into the earth, and the sound of the dirt being cast off from the shovels, landing in a growing mound behind Henry and Pa. Side by side, they continued to wordlessly tend to the urgent job in front of them. Together they created a final resting place for Roger, in a grave, next to the majestic maple, on the top of Walker Hill.

Chapter 45:

They arrived by car and on foot. The good people of Wilton filed into the field behind the Rowe house without pomp or circumstance. There had been no obituary or article in the local newspaper. It was by word of mouth, and that was enough to bring friends, family and the classmates of Roger and his sisters.

By the time it was 2:00, Laura imagined the whole village of Wilton had relocated itself on Walker Hill to say goodbye to Roger, her brother, and a fallen war hero. There were no seats or tents. Everyone simply gathered in a half circle around Roger's open grave. The only chair was placed next to where Pa stood, and that chair was for Ma.

Several of Roger's friends and cousins emerged from the house carrying Roger's casket on their shoulders. Quietly, they marched toward the gravesite, as Henry walked behind them. For the first time in almost four years, Henry wore his minister's robe and prayer shawl, and carried his Bible.

His voice strong and full of conviction, Henry began and the crowd followed suit: "O Lord my God, when I so awesome wonder, Consider all the worlds Thy hands have made: I see the stars, I hear the rolling thunder, Thy power throughout the universe displayed..."

Laura's eyes burned with pride and tears at the sight and sound of her husband's strong voice. Yes, there he was when she needed him most. In one hand was her daughter's tiny hand, and her other hand rested on her son's sloping shoulder. The music trailed into the air, and it seemed to Laura as if the sound could certainly reach heaven easily enough from the top of this great hill.

"Then sings my soul, my Savior God, to Thee," and with great force Laura could hear Pa's baritone voice over everyone's, "How great Thou art! How great Thou art!" Laura could see Pa's hand on Ma's heaving shoulder, and she watched Ma reach up to pat her husband's sturdy hand. "Then sings my soul, My Savoir God, to Thee, How great Thou art! How great Thou art!"

Somehow on that hot August afternoon, the family managed to say goodbye to Roger. Henry ended the service with a prayer and those who wished, tossed a shovelful of dirt into the grave. When the final guest said farewell, some of Roger's friends remained behind to help Pa finish covering the grave with the rich soil of Walker Hill.

After the service, incredibly, like the loaves of bread in the Bible feeding the massive hoards, the entire crowd was fed from the tiny Walker Hill kitchen and single wood stove which had burned hot all day. After a bountiful meal, served on a hodgepodge of odds and ends of bone china dishes collected over several generations, people shared their stories and said their goodbyes, and the hill was quiet once again.

That evening, Ma and Pa closed their tired eyes knowing their son had returned to Walker Hill.

Chapter 46:

Laura's older sister Ruth lived just outside of Wilton, in the thriving mill town of Rumford. Ruth's husband, Arthur, was a mill worker, and occasionally he would have business that would require him to pass through Wilton. Whenever such an occasion arrived, Arthur would have Ruth and their three–year-old daughter, Jan-Jan, join him so he could drop them off on Walker Hill for the day.

Ruth was always overjoyed to get to spend the day with Ma and Pa, but she was especially happy when Laura moved in with her parents, so she could spend the day, not only with her parents, but with her sister, and her niece and nephew, too.

Rose was just old enough to love watching over Jannie. Little Jan just adored playing with her older cousin, Rose. Rose would spend hours taking Jan by the hand and gently leading her around the farm to peek in at the chickens and perhaps pluck an egg or two from a nest. Jan also was content to just sit and play with Ma's pots and pans or gather cups and saucers to play tea party with Rose, her happy servant, who would joyfully bring her dishes and tiny nibbles of Ma's kitchen treats as Jan commanded. Both girls had long brown ringlets surrounding their lovely little faces. They had matching pairs of big brown, almond shaped eyes and long black veils of lashes. The girls looked more like sisters than cousins.

Laura looked so forward to the days Ruth would come to the farm, and over time, Rose, desperate for a playmate besides Norman who paid her no mind whatsoever, would ask for days on end, "When will Jannie be coming again?" Everyone looked forward to the arrival of Baby Jan and Aunt Ruth.

On one particular visit, in late autumn, as Ruth and Laura and Ma shared a rare quiet moment and sipped tea and mindlessly chatted about Wilton townspeople, Rose walked in with little Jannie in tow, as usual. "Auntie Ruth," Rose said earnestly, interrupting the grown ups' visit, looking up at her aunt. "What's wrong with Jannie's eye?"

Her innocent question prompted all three women to stop their conversation and look down at Jan. Ruth bent down as Rose pointed at Jan's left eye, and as Jan looked up at her Momma, Laura and Ma could see the color completely and absolutely drain out of Ruth's handsome face. Jan's left eye remained fixed in one corner. Ma could see Ruth's panic, and she grabbed her daughter's hand and took over so as not to panic little Jan.

"Come now, come now Jan Jan," Ma crooned to her little granddaughter, "Let's have a look here at your old Granny now," but Jannie's eye remained fixed in that same spot. Her right eye looked directly at her Granny as was requested, but her left eye didn't move at all. Ma plucked Jannie up and held her on her hip, never taking her gaze off Jan's left eye.

Ruth looked pleadingly at Ma for an answer, but Ma simply said calmly, "Well now, let's get Pa to bring his wagon round. Jannie needs to go see Dr. Bennings in town."

"Should we wait for Arthur to get here? Should we wait and bring her to Rumford?" Ruth asked in a shaky voice, measuring Ma's response to weigh just how much she should be panicking.

Ma was calm, but blunt and abrupt. "Jan needs to see a doctor now Ruthie. He'll know what to do."

Laura rushed to her sister's side when she saw Ruth's eyes fill with tears. She didn't want little Jannie to be afraid, so she pulled her sister's hand with her toward the door, "Let's go get Pa, Ruthie," and the girls ran off leaving Jannie with Ma and Rose.

Pa hitched the horses to the wagon promptly when his daughters found him in the field and told him about Little Jannie's eye. Ma, Pa, Jannie and Ruth left post haste, leaving behind a somber lot. Henry, Norman, Rose and Laura stood at the top of Walker Hill watching the wagon disappear over the steep slope of the hill.

Chapter 47:

Dr. Bennings made an immediate appointment for Jannie to go to Maine Medical Center in Portland, the largest hospital in Maine. Even though Ruth was the older sister, she asked Laura to go with her since Laura had the experience of bringing Normy to Boston to the hospital.

Ma decided to send Pa, so she could remain behind at Walker Hill to help Henry with Norman, and to tend little Rose.

And so it was. Pa and Laura packed an overnight bag and drove off with Arthur and Ruth and baby Jan. Just like that. The day had become something so different from how it had began.

Little Jan sat, happily, between Pa and her Aunt Laura. Laura threaded her fingers between Jannie's tiny fingers, and held them there feeling the warmth of her impossibly small hand. Laura looked down to see Pa's fingers twirling through Jan's mass of curls. Arthur drove without speaking. Ruth quietly repeated, "Dr. Bennings thinks it is an easy fix for the doctors in Portland. It's probably just an easy fix." Everyone nodded in agreement. A few miles later, Ruth would repeat her mantra, and again, everyone would nod. "Yes, it will be an easy fix for the doctors in Portland."

Jannie sat contentedly between her Auntie Laura and Pa-Pa. She looked adoringly from one to the other, jouncing along in the back of her Daddy's car. Her angelic smile indicated she had no idea that the tension filling the automobile had anything to do with her. That was just how they wanted it to be. Laura could not un-see the fixed eye looking back at her when she looked down at her beautiful niece.

Could this tiny imperfection in her niece's lovely symmetrical face be dangerous? It seemed unimaginable.

Chapter 48:

The solemn team of doctors who met Arthur, Ruth, Laura and Pa downplayed Jannie's fixed eye. They disclosed that it was most likely a tumor, but in recounting the conversation, Laura remembered them making it sound as if they see this sort of problem regularly. In Laura's mind, they made it sound as common as the common cold.

As Arthur, Ruth and Pa sat in the waiting room with Laura, they were worried, but not nearly as worried as they should have been.

The four adults surrounded Jannie's stretcher as it was being pushed into surgery. They all loved on Little Jan up right until she was rolled into the operating room. Hugs, handholding, squeezes, blown kisses, and final affections were delivered all the way up the hallway. Little Jan's body was no more than a slight whisper beneath the sheets; she looked so tiny as she was rolled down the long, sterile hallway. She sweetly blew one final kiss in her family's direction as she was whisked through the double doors into the surgical suite.

Ruth and Laura held hands tightly as they bravely blew kisses back to brave Little Jannie. Gloved and capped surgeons and nurses followed just behind Jannie's cot, and the doors shut behind them. And then, she disappeared.

Laura could feel Ruth's whole body quaking. She squeezed her sister's ice cold hand tightly.

"Well," Pa drawled as the tight group of four gathered in the waiting room, "I guess Little Jan is in about the best hands there is," and they all nodded solemnly. As the hours passed, the group recounted statements they had heard before Jannie went into surgery.

"They said they thought the tumor was benign," Laura whispered. "That's good."

Arthur nodded, "Ya, that's real good."

Ruth moved closer to Arthur, "Yes, it's the best we can hope for." Arthur put his arm protectively around Ruth's shoulder, and Pa noticed, pleased his daughter was married to a man who was strong when he needed to be.

Pa moved from one chair to the next in the waiting room. Laura had never seen her father indoors for such a long stretch of time, unless he was sound asleep in the evening. Sometimes, after a hard day's work outdoors, he would sit in his rocking chair, and nod off next to the woodstove, open Bible in his lap. Pa was inside only for a meal or for a quick chat, and then he would move right back out to the fields or the barn. Pa looked so out of place to Ruth and Laura, caged in this waiting room hour after hour.

Was it six? Was it seven hours later? Gosh it had been forever. Finally, a doctor came through the waiting room doors. His mask hung below his chin, and he was pulling his gloves from his hands. Without comment, everyone in the room moved to their feet and toward the doctor. Arthur reached him first. Ruth was directly behind.

The doctor's expression was grim. Ruth saw this immediately and lurched forward.

Laura heard his words, but they sounded as if they may have come from the depths of the ocean. She felt as if she was hearing the news from the bottom of the sea. "It was much worse than we thought," the doctor began. Laura reached for Pa's hands. Pa's hands reached back. They were ice cold.

Ruth didn't wait for the next words. Her sobs came from the bottom of her soul. "We could not save her," the doctor continued painfully. "She's gone," he flatly ended.

All Laura remembered were Ruth's arms. Instinctively she raised her arms both up toward the doctor. She lifted them there in front of him. Her arms just hung there, reaching, reaching. She was reaching for her little girl. She held them there. Her eyes never left the doctor as she stood there waiting. Waiting for Jannie. Waiting for the familiar weight of her little girl to fill them.

Arthur moved toward Ruth but she just kept her arms right there, empty arms reaching for her little Jannie.

Ruth's head shook back and forth, no. "No," she whispered, empty arms still held in the air. "No, no, no," and her girl was gone. Just like that.

Laura collapsed into Pa's arms. She couldn't look at her sister any longer. Not like that. Not with her haunted eyes and those empty arms reaching for a little girl that would never again run into them.

Chapter 49:

Never was there a more peaceful time on Walker Hill than in the dead of winter. In the evening, the only sounds were those of the unforgiving winds at the top of the hill, swirling and battering their strength against the insolent determination of the farm.

Nighttime came early in the winter. Once the sun set behind the barn, and the evening dishes were done, the family would gather in the sitting room, the warmest room in the house. On most nights, Ma would be knitting, embroidering or stitching holiday gifts in her cane backed rocking chair. Pa would be next to Norman's wheelchair, quietly reading the prose of a favorite poet or verses from the Bible. Norman was soothed by the lilt of Pa's steady voice. Henry had his easel set up in the corner of the sitting room, and he would quietly dab his brush into the oils on his palate and swipe the paint across the canvas, the creations in his mind coming to life beneath his paintbrush for all to enjoy.

Laura would frequently just sit. While the others were immersed in their hobbies, to Laura just sitting and being still was what she craved. As the adults around her dabbled with their crafts and hobbies, Laura preferred to sip a piping hot cup of tea and enjoy the predictability of the evening's structure.

It seemed impossible to Laura that her own life, so small and insignificant in the scheme of things, had delivered so many heartbreaking blows. When Norman was born, she first tasted the bitter pill of a life altering event, so outside of her control or even outside of her imagining. She had such a healthy pregnancy, and then her boy was born so damaged, and that it seemed, created a cataclysmic domino effect of loss that Laura could not alter.

Norman's seizures and disability seemed to be more than Henry could accept, so Laura lost Henry...and then Henry lost his job. It was then that Laura lost her home, and when she moved back to Walker Hill, Laura lost her way. Her compass went spinning, temporarily, and she lost her true north.

And once back on Walker Hill, they all lost in the most permanent and unforgiving sense. They lost Roger and, no sooner than Roger died, precious Little Jannie's death followed.

So many brutal blows were sustained atop of Walker Hill. And so, in the evening, when all was calm and the house was tidied and the children were made ready for bed, Laura just sat. The predictability and serenity of each evening, was all she wanted. It was what her soul needed.

Outside the winds howled their way up the hill. Inside the fires crackled in the fireplaces and in the woodstove. Every now and then a log would shift and tumble inside of the belly of the stove. The candlelight flickered inside of the hurricane lamps, casting wild shadows across the farmhouse walls. The woodsy scents of balsam and cinnamon fragranced the air. The lilt of Pa's voice was music in Laura's ears.

She wished things could stay exactly this way forever.

Chapter 50:

After both Jan and Roger's funerals, it seemed at times as if sorrow itself hung low and sure over the crest of Walker Hill. Jan had been little Rose's best friend, and as much as the adults were feeling the presence of the loss of that child, all were aware that Rose was broken hearted too. It seemed more important than ever to find ways for Rose to spend time with other children her age.

Little Rose had the chance to meet some local new friends during Roger's service. One kind neighbor offered to bring Rose to Wilson Lake for swimming lessons with their daughter. Rose had just turned five, and most of her years, all that she could remember, had been spent on the farm on Walker Hill, so she was both wildly excited to join a friend for swimming lessons and terribly nervous at the same time.

Although never cold nor hungry on the farm, there was never extra. Ma and Laura had made all of Rose's clothes, and often on the hottest days of the year, Rose just ran free and wild in her underwear and t-shirt, barefoot and unabashed, talking with the animals and playing among the rows of vegetables and the fields.

When the time came for swimming lessons, Laura realized with a start that Rose did not have a swimming costume. She went to Ma with the situation about an hour before Rose's ride was due to pick her up.

"Well," Ma pondered, "that shouldn't be a problem. We can rig something up for her," and Ma went to work.

Ma found a woolen, plaid scarf in a drawer and fashioned a hook so she could place the scarf around Rose's tiny chest and clasp it shut. She pulled it around Rose and Rose squirmed and scowled when she felt the itchiness of the wool against her skin. Laura looked concerned and uncertain about the garment Ma had selected, and Ma just said, "Well that will just have to do," gruffly and left no room for question.

"What about her bottoms?" Laura said as she looked Rose over. "She's going to need a bathing suit bottom."

"Well, she's a tiny little thing, so what do we have here?" Ma said as she rummaged through the drawers of a bureau in the back bedroom. "Well looky here," Ma said happily as she held up a pair of tiny plaid shorts from, most likely, Laura's childhood, almost thirty years ago. She pulled the shorts up over Rose's little hips, but they were way too big and they kept slipping off. Ma scowled, and Rose looked up at her mother with a worried expression on her face.

Ma went into the kitchen and came back victoriously holding up a frayed old rope. "This should do the trick," she said as she threaded the rope through the belt loops and wrapped the rope around Rose's waist and tied it, snuggly holding the shorts into place. Ma stood back and took it in, "We did it, with not a moment to spare," she declared proudly.

Laura took in the appearance of her little girl and felt dismayed and more than a bit concerned. Little Rose looked like a rag tag urchin in her roped up shorts and itchy scarf, makeshift bathing suit. Ma flapped her hand in disgust toward Laura, and muttered under her breath about the evils of vanity. Laura attempted to come around, because she certainly didn't want Rose to worry. "Well there, little one. You are all set for your first swimming lessons," she said with artificial cheerfulness, and she handed Rose a stiff and scratchy terrycloth towel fresh from the clothesline.

When Rose's ride arrived, Laura could plainly see by the looks on the little girls' faces inside of the car that Rose was going to stick out like a sore thumb at her swimming lessons at Wilson Lake. Apologetically, Laura whispered a sorry explanation to the girls' mother as she ushered Rose into the back seat of the car. The mother nodded politely but appeared a bit perplexed as she took in Rose's sorry–excuse- for- a -bathing suit. Laura could not get the sight of her daughter's worried face out of her mind as the car drove off and down over Walker Hill.

It was in that moment, with crystal clarity, that Laura decided to approach Henry about returning to the ministry. As much as she loved and adored her life, connected to her cherished homeland, on the top of Walker Hill, she did not want her children to grow up as poor as a raggedy band of church mice. Instead, she knew in that very defining moment, she wanted to return to life as a minister's wife

back in the church.

Chapter 51:

It was just as Laura worried it would be. Rose came back from Wilson Lake never having dipped a single toe into the water. As young as she was, she noticed right away that she looked different from the other children, and she told the swim instructor she had a tummy ache. She sat on the side of the dock and watched the other children, in bathing suits and bathing caps, jumping in and out of the water. She half roasted in her scratchy wool top and shorts, and the mother who had given her a ride never offered again.

This just would not do. Laura was heartsick when little Rose recounted the story to her at bedtime. Just before falling asleep, as Laura rubbed her daughter's forehead, Rose asked, "Mommy. One day may I have one of those swimsuits and caps like the other children have?"

Laura's eyes burned with tears and she assured her daughter that indeed one day she would have a fine bathing suit and a bathing cap to match. Rose told her mother that she would prefer a pink bathing suit and a yellow cap, and Laura quickly agreed that pink and yellow would be an ideal combination. Pleased and taking her mother for her word, Rose nodded off to sleep, but Laura didn't sleep a wink that night.

Laura tossed and turned and recounted the story that brought her back to Walker Hill. She thought back to the time when she had first met Henry. He was ten years her senior, and had just come back from seminary school in Bangor, Maine.

Laura hated every minute of her formal schooling, from grade school to high school. When she met Henry, she had just graduated from high school and she wanted nothing more than to leave Walker Hill. Handsome and smart, Henry swept Laura right off from her feet. Henry was older, smarter, and he had lived "away." She had barely ever been outside of Wilton. She couldn't wait to marry him and move away from her life on Walker Hill.

She thought he would take care of her for her entire life. But then Norman was born, and it seemed Henry could barely even take care of himself. The life she had imagined with Henry, was not the life she was leading.

She thought, then, of Ma. She had been on this hill with Pa for her whole life. She never seemed one way or another. She just was always the same. She raised four babies on this hill...with no running water, no indoor plumbing, no electricity, and yet, she never complained. Laura couldn't once remember Ma complaining. Once in a while, she would point out to Pa in the fields, reciting his poetry, but she would just chuckle, and say, "Look at that dreamer out there. Such a dreamer," and she would just smile and continue rolling out the dough, preparing buttermilk biscuits for the evening meal.

Staring into the night, Laura recalled Ma's words, "Show me where it says you need to be happy in the Bible." Was Ma happy? Laura wondered.

But then Laura remembered the moment Ma found out Roger died. She remembered Pa going straight to Ma, and Ma holding on to him as if her life depended on it. Her eyes watered picturing the way they clung to each other, as if either would crumble into the earth if one let go.

In the pitch darkness of their bedroom on the farm, Laura reached her hand out to find her husband in the blackness. She found his back and laid her hand there, feeling tenderness toward him as he breathed in and out. Her father's words played out in her mind as she remembered the pain in Henry's eyes the day he walked out of his church: "Every man has his secret sorrows which the world knows not; and often times we call a man cold when he is only sad."

On the day of Roger's funeral, Henry rose to the occasion, quite literally. He dusted off his minister's robe, wore it proudly and, most importantly, he found the words to bring solace and comfort to all of her brother's people. He would be a minister again. This Laura knew to be true. She closed her eyes and fell asleep next to her husband.

Chapter 52:

Hildy pulled up to the front porch and stomped her foot hard onto the emergency brake. "My Christ Lord and Savior," she sputtered. "This damned hill is going to be the end of this car," and she got out to load up the trunk with the suitcases on the porch. "Let's get this show on the road," she hollered to anyone who was listening, but it was a tearful lot standing in front of her, huddling together in emotional goodbyes.

Ma tucked a few precious dollars in Laura's hand, whispering to her to find someone in her new town to get her hair done for Henry's first day of preaching. "Everyone's gonna be looking to see the new minister's wife, Laura. Give them something to look at," she said with a wink.

"Ma," Laura answered with a smile, "I thought vanity was wicked."

"It's only wicked when I say it's wicked," Ma said with a laugh.

Little Rose climbed into the back of the car with a giant smile on her face. It was always a treat to get a chance to ride in any car, she had done so so rarely; therefore, she was ready to go. Henry made mention, loud enough for Hildy to hear, that Rose had been too young to remember the last ride with Aunt Hildy or she would not be nearly so anxious for this to get underway. At that, Hildy delivered a playful swat to her brother's arm.

Pa picked up Norman, and placed him in the car next to his mother, who was scrunched in the middle between her two children. Once Norman was safely in, Pa slammed the car door shut. His weathered face was filled with raw emotion, and he wiped his eyes on the sleeve of his flannel shirt. Henry gave Pa a firm handshake, and sounded embarrassed as he thanked him for sharing his home and caring for his family for so many years.

Pa brushed away the thanks, and sounded sincere as he thanked Henry for the help with the farm. Henry hurriedly got into the front seat next to his sister as she revved up the motor. "God help us," he said out the window to Ma and Pa as Hildy's tires spun gravel as she began down over the hill. Laura had Rose blowing kisses out the back window until they could no longer see Ma and Pa standing there waving, through the dust.

Ma openly cried as she watched Laura's little family disappear down over Walker Hill. "I don't know what I'm gonna do with myself now," she said quietly to Pa.

"Oh we managed before. We will manage again," and they both turned back to the house and went slowly in opposite directions to tend to their chores.

Chapter 53:

Laura wiped tears away from the corners of her eyes as Walker Hill vanished from view. As the car careened through the center of town, she saw the storefront of the Sears and Roebuck. Laura's face burned at the memory of her secret memories. She closed her eyes remembering the photograph, Matthew's kiss, the afternoon in Matthew's truck.

Laura looked directly in front of her, at the back of her husband's head. She wondered anxiously what he would think of her if he knew she had been vain, and had been unfaithful. She silently shook her head. It was such a stupid thing to do, she thought.

But, she wasn't certain if she regretted it.

As the car rolled on, Laura wondered what was in store for her little family. Henry had met with the leaders of the church, and they readily placed him into a little country church in a town 30 minutes away from Livermore. He would be the minister of The United Methodist Church in Mechanic Falls. It was a sweet, tiny wooden church, bright inside with paned glass windows, and with a proud steeple in the center. Laura loved it upon first sight, and she felt as if Henry did too.

Henry was excited and flattered that the church elders were so pleased that he would be returning to the ministry. They felt his personal experience with melancholia may actually make him a stronger minister, more empathetic and more understanding of the human experience. He agreed that he did indeed have a deeper awareness of how life's trials can impact your faith, your spirituality and your belief system.

Henry could frequently be heard saying, "Trust in the Lord with all your heart and lean not on your own understanding in all your ways, acknowledge him and he will direct your path." He said it quietly, under his breath, at all different times throughout the day, as if convincing his own self that the words were so. He whispered it as he pushed Norman's wheelchair, or when he hoed the gardens, or when he mucked out the barn floor.

Laura wondered sometimes. Did the Lord direct her path to spend time with Matthew? Was that the work of the Lord or the devil? Did it have to be one or the other? Maybe both. She was perplexed. Laura spent hours ruminating with this thought. As she spooned Ma's custard into Norman's mouth, she would daydream about that day when she had her photograph taken. As she gently guided the spoon toward Norman, she wondered if she would have known or recognized her love and commitment toward Henry if she not been tempted by Matthew.

She remembered the day when she, exhausted from the walk, crested the hill and saw Henry sitting on the blanket, in the bright sunshine, with Norman by his side. Henry was playing the harmonica and it was as if the music was injected directly into her heart. In that very moment, she knew she loved her husband. "For better or for worse," and they had certainly known both.

The car drove on, and Laura grew more and more excited for her new life to begin. She smiled to herself as Henry barked out the directions to the new parsonage to his impatient sister in the driver's seat. "Sharp left Hildy," and the car careened sideways barely missing the curb of the sidewalk. Henry gripped the handle of the door, and Laura protectively grabbed hold of Norman and Rose.

"A little notice might be nice Reverend," Hildy hissed back at her brother.

Laura straightened the children in their seats and somehow felt all was right with her world.

Chapter 54:

That feeling did not last long.

Once again, Laura fell in love with her little parsonage. She spent every spare moment decorating and fussing over the appearance of her new home. She certainly missed Ma's help with the children, but it was lovely to have her own home again. And it was nice to have some privacy.

She couldn't remember being intimate with Henry more than once or maybe twice in all of the years that they spent with Ma and Pa. At first he was in his deepest depression, and she couldn't reach him. Once the clouds lifted, their room was too close to Ma and Pa to feel comfortable. Now, Laura felt ignited by the freedom of being alone as a little family.

Laura had missed her monthly, and was thrilled to think she may be starting out in a new church with another baby on the way. One early morning as she fought off a bit of nausea, she tied a bright blue gingham apron around her waist and began cracking eggs into a yellow ware bowl. She whisked the eggs until they were frothy before pouring them, sputtering noisily, into piping hot bacon grease in the bottom of the skillet. She rolled Norman's wheelchair to the table and yelled to Henry and Rose that breakfast would be ready soon.

And then, that very bright, cheerful morning, as she was feeding Norman his scrambled eggs, Norman's teeth clenched down on the spoon, and his back arched, as if he had been electrocuted, at an impossible angle.

Laura, startled, and attempted to pull the spoon out of Normy's mouth, but she was no match against the grip his jaw held down on the utensil. "Henry," she screamed, leaping from her chair and wrapping her arm around Norman's head. "Help, Henry," and her husband, came running around the corner looking in horror at Normy.

It had been nearly a decade since they had battled a seizure, and Norman, naturally, was much larger and heavier. Henry awkwardly picked his rigid form up from the wheelchair and placed him, as carefully as he could, on the braided rug on the kitchen floor.

Laura was scared to death he would swallow the spoon, and she tried to hold it in place in his frothing mouth until at last he released his clenched jaw. Henry tried to protect his son's head from beating against the floor as Norman jerked and arched, and quaked for an unimaginably long time. His forehead was burning with heat, when finally he stopped and looking dazed, fell into a deep sleep.

Laura and Henry, both crouched low on either side of their boy on the floor, caught each other's terrified gaze. Tears spilled down Laura's cheeks as she stroked her handsome boy's face. "Oh my boy, my poor, poor Normy," she repeated over and over and over again as he breathed raggedly, in his bone weary slumber.

Laura looked up at Henry, and with a ferocity, unfamiliar to even her, she said evenly, "You are not going anywhere Henry," and he met her gaze. "You are staying right here with me through this...whatever this is."

Henry started to interrupt, "Laura, I..." his voice catching.

"You will be right by my side Henry," her eyes piercing his as her voice began raising loudly, "whatever happens."

And she stood and saw little Rose standing in the corner of the kitchen, tears staining both of her rosy cheeks. She had witnessed the terrifying seizure. Laura went to her little girl and soothed her, smoothing her hair, "It's okay honey. Normy's okay, it was very scary, but he's okay," and in the back of her mind she wondered if she was telling her little girl the truth.

Suddenly nothing felt okay.

Henry picked up Norman and brought him upstairs to sleep off the effects of the seizure. He pulled up the gate next to Normy's twin mattress, keeping him safely on his bed without a chance of him rolling to the floor.

He and Laura spent so much of their time keeping him safe. Carefully pinning his diapers away from his flesh, so he never would get an accidental poke from the pins, belting him around the waist in his wheelchair so he would never pitch forward and get a bump on the head. They blew hot stews and porridges cool before bringing the spoon to Norman's lips. They tended every rash, every tooth, every fingernail, every toe and yet, they always knew in some ways, they could not keep him safe at all.

After placing Norman on his bed, Henry returned to the kitchen where Laura still held Rose, and he took them both into his arms. He rocked back and forth lightly and repeated, "Trust in the Lord with all your heart and lean not on your own understanding in all your ways, acknowledge him and he will direct your path." And Laura knew Henry wasn't going anywhere this time.

Chapter 55:

Once the seizures started, there was no end. They were daily and violent and terrifying. Although Henry never retreated, he had the escape of going to church, of meetings, of the daily life of a minister.

Laura stood in the window as Henry left the house, watching him head to the church for whatever meeting might be held that morning, and she felt jealous. Once again, he got to get away. Laura felt a hostage to her home, to her children, to Norman's seizures.

Laura never left the parsonage for fear Norman would have a seizure. How would she manage in a grocery store or in a neighbor's kitchen. Here, in her parsonage next to the church, she could have Rose run to get Henry next door, day or night.

On her best days, she would cheerfully tend her home and her children. She would sew Rose dresses for school, she would crochet doilies for her dinner table, she would bake breads and make jams, and fill her little home with delicious scents. She would hum tunes from the Methodist hymnal.

But on her worst days, seizure days, she would stare out the window and watch the whole world seem to pass her by. She felt caged in by the walls of her home. She felt trapped by her son. She would stare at the jagged scar on the side of his head, beneath his neat crew cut Henry gave him, and she would curse that brain that held her whole world captive.

On her best days, she would sing quietly to Norman as she brought the spoon to his lips, "If I knew you were coming I'd of baked a cake, baked a cake, baked a cake, howd ya do, howd ya do, howd ya do… " and Rose would sing along with her at the table, laughing next to her Mommy.

On her worst days, Laura would raise the spoon in stony silence, wishing she were back in Wilton. Wishing she could smell the air of Walker Hill, wishing Ma were the one with the spoon, and she had another day to run carefree down the hill filling her lungs with air and the taste of freedom. On her worst days, every chore seemed too much. Every act became a burden.

And then one bright October day, with the sun shining and the sky so blue it dazzled as the back drop to Maine's tapestry of autumn leaves, Norman died.

Chapter 56:

Ma and Pa arrived from Walker Hill in Aunt Hildy's car. No words were exchanged when they entered the house. Laura simply went to her mother and let her mother hold her. No words were necessary, as Ma knew full well the pain of burying a child.

Aunt Hildy spewed some words out in Laura's direction, her awkward attempt at being a comforting presence, and she then walked over to her brother who was sitting at the kitchen table. She placed her hand on his, and for her brother, she was a comforting presence. She held her hand there, and he let her.

Pa pulled a handkerchief from his trousers and brusquely wiped away some unwelcome tears as he looked away from his wife and daughter's embrace. Pa noticed Norman's empty wheelchair in the corner of the kitchen. He moved toward it, to move it out, hoping somehow not seeing the wheelchair could lessen everyone's pain. As he bent to unlock the brakes, both Laura and Henry rose instinctively toward him.

"No," Laura shouted, surprising even herself. "No, don't..."

Pa looked embarrassed, as he stuttered, "I thought maybe..." and Henry interrupted.

"Just leave it. Just go ahead and leave it," the broken words Henry was able to utter. And he repeated, with his hand on Pa's arm. "Please, just leave it."

Pa moved away from Norman's wheelchair, and steadily said, "Of course, of course I will," and Pa walked out to the front porch to collect himself.

Ma still held Laura, crooning now to her, "Oh my poor girl. My poor, poor Laura," and Laura clung to her mother.

Who would she be? Laura wondered as she stood swaying in her mother's arms. Who would she be without her boy? What would she be, if not Norman's mother?

And a final thought occurred to her, "And why would she be?"

Chapter 57:

Why would she be?

Laura had no idea what to do with herself without her boy. For sixteen years, her days and her nights belonged to him. She rose in the morning and as soon as she had dressed herself, she dressed Norman. As soon as she had taken a sip of tea, she began giving him sips of milk or juice. If a bite went to her mouth, a bite went to his. If she wiped her own lips, she would wipe his. Even if she went to the bathroom, she would change his diaper, knowing he must have gone too.

Who was she now? She was as familiar with his daily patterns as she was her own. Without the rhythm of his day, she had lost the rhythm of her own.

Little Rose was off to school, so the house was empty. And every corner of the house brought to mind her Norman.

All of the things Laura wanted to do when Norman was alive, she no longer wanted to do. When Norman was alive, she would stare out the window at the world outside. Then, she longed to go for a long walk, or leisurely peruse the aisles of a store, or visit a friend, or she dreamed about taking peaceful, solitary walks on a sandy shore. Now Laura had the freedom to do all of these things, but she no longer found pleasure in the thought of doing any of them.

And worse still, as happy as she had been, prior to Norman's death, to know she was having another baby, her happiness turned to sorrow and guilt. She felt she was trading one life for another.

Henry watched his wife cautiously. He recognized the warning signs of pulling away from life, and he saw his wife beginning to disappear from him and from Rose. She robotically sat Rose's breakfast in front of her, and packed her lunch, and kissed her on top of her head when she shooed her out the door for school, but there was no attachment, no emotion. She just was.

Laura returned to church, but instead of proudly sitting in the front row with Rose next to her, she chose the back pew, and rarely, if ever looked up to the pulpit. She stood during the hymns, but never moved her lips, never raised her voice. He remembered the joy she used to emanate when she sang, along with the congregation, all of the hymns of her childhood. But now, if the songs stirred her, they stirred only pain.

One day, after the leaves from the trees had all fallen leaving the skeletal remains of bare branches silhouetting the landscape. Just before the arrival of the several feet of Maine winter snow blanketing the earth, Henry surprised Laura with the arrival of none other than, Aunt Hildy.

Aunt Hildy's Oldsmobile pulled up into the driveway of the parsonage just before Rose was ready to trudge off to school. Rose and Laura exchanged shocked expressions as a bent and stooped Aunt Hildy rapped on the door. "Ding dong, taxi's here," Aunt Hildy joked as she pushed her way into the kitchen.

"Well, what on earth?" Laura asked looking genuinely perplexed toward Henry.

Henry rose from his seat and with a twinkle in his eye, he said, "I thought maybe a trip to Walker Hill would do my girls some good," and he put his arm around his wife as he gently said this.

"Yayyyyyyyy!!" little Rose jumped up and down. "I want to go," and she flung her brown bag lunch on the table, running to her father with gratitude.

"Henry, what about school?" Laura asked, looking at her excited daughter.

"School, shmool," Hildy spat out. "This kid needs some fresh air and some of her Grandmother's cooking by the looks," and as she said this, Laura took in her little girl, pale and nervous. She hadn't even noticed before.

"Laura, Thanksgiving Break is next week. Let Rose take a little extra time off. It'll do you both a world of good."

Laura glanced around. This surprise had thrown her all off course, and she didn't know quite what to do.   Aunt Hildy tapped her foot impatiently, "Chop, chop," she said urging Laura to begin packing. Laura's glance caught the image of Norman's wheelchair still sitting in the corner of the kitchen. She kept her gaze there, as she said, "Okay, then. Okay," and she backed up away from them all, "I'll go pack at once."

She turned away from Norman's chair and headed to her bedroom to pack. Henry and Aunt Hildy exchanged relieved looks as Laura took off her apron and grabbed a suitcase from the hall closet.

Chapter 58:

Ma practically ran down the driveway to pull Laura out of Hildy's car. Ma hadn't laid eyes on her daughter Laura since Norman's funeral. She put her arms around Laura and was shocked at the amount of weight she had lost. The only weight she held appeared to be the tiniest bump in Laura's abdomen. When she grabbed little Rose out of the back seat, she clucked at how pale and thin her granddaughter was as well. She was determined to change that in a hurry!

Before Laura pulled her suitcase out of Aunt Hildy's trunk, she looked out on the barren hill. The fields of Walker Hill were filled with cat-o'-ninetails and milk pods, and decaying remnants of wild flowers that had been brilliant just weeks before. Soon these fields would be covered with snow and ice and the unforgiving cold of winter.

But then, as was the pattern of nature, Laura knew next spring, the seeds will have sown themselves, the blooms would reach for the sun, and all would be in full bloom again. The hills would be splendid with the brilliant colors of wild flowers: purple lupine, tiny blue forget-me-nots, pure white daisies with golden centers, specks of white and green lily of the valley, bright orange Indian paintbrushes, golden brown-eyed Susans with giant chestnut centers. They would surely all bloom, coming alive and transforming this giant hill.

Laura put her hand on her abdomen, where her new baby was beginning to quicken inside of her. She yanked her suitcase from the trunk and turned to the weathered and worn steps of her childhood and the faded yellow front door. Pa stood, just where she knew he would be, waving to her from the doorway.

Holding onto her mother's hand, she stepped into the kitchen with the dozens of squares of mismatched wallpaper. She saw color for the first time in months.

Chapter 59:

Ma, oven mitts in hand, pulled the enormous bird out of the Heartland cookstove oven and began to ladel the golden juices over the turkey to baste it. The kitchen was fragranced with the scents of turkey and sage, sweet potato and brown sugar, and Ma's delicious rising yeast rolls. Rose, bundled in her winter coat, was outside with Pa, scattering seeds to feed the chickens and running around teasing the goats. Her cheeks were pink from the cold.

Once Ma shoved the pan back into the oven, she stood and mopped her brow, sweat beaded from the exertion of a morning filled with the preparations for Thanksgiving. Laura was grateful for the time alone with Ma, working side by side in the tiny kitchen.

"Ma," Laura began slowly, "Do you remember that day when you sent me into town to get my hair done at The Clip and Curl?"

Ma thought for a split second, and answered, "Well, sure, I guess I do remember that day. I took the money out of my secret jar," she said with a conspiratorial smile and a look toward Pa outside.

"I wasn't used to being off by myself Ma. I wasn't used to having my hair all fancy," Laura took a breath and continued. Ma paused for a moment to look at Laura as she went on. "My life was so small then. It was all about Norman, and Henry wasn't well, and Rose was a toddler."

"Oh yes, I remember. It was a hard time for you Laura. That's why I sent you off, to give you a little treat," Ma said matter of factly.

"Well, I should never have gone. The hairdo. The time by myself. It all went to my head," Laura said. Ma looked at her puzzled.

Then Ma said sharply, "Laura. What are you trying to tell me? Just say it."

Laura took a deep breath and her eyes welled with tears at the memory. "I did something I shouldn't have done Ma," she said remembering her kiss with Matthew, "and I think God took Normy to punish me."

"Well, what in hell did you do Laura? Did you kill someone?" Ma said clearly exasperated by trying to guess. "Did you kill a man when you were downtown getting your hair done?"

Laura dabbed at the tears in her eyes, and turned to her mother ready to make a full confession to alleviate the guilt she had felt for some years now. "I kissed a man Ma. I kissed the photographer."

Ma looked fairly stunned at what Laura was saying. "You kissed the photographer? Well how the Jiminy Cricket did that happen?" Ma said while going back to the sink to peel some carrots. "Tell me the whole darned story Laura."

So, Laura did. She told her mother how she had felt when she ran down the hill, the thrill she felt when she turned in the beauty parlor chair to see her chestnut hair all done up. She explained to her mother how the beautician took some extra time to make Laura up to look like a Hollywood star with make up and a swipe of gorgeous red lipstick. Ma listened intently.

Laura watched outside as Rose and Pa held hands on the way to the woodshed, and she wiped a stray tear away from the corner of her eye as she explained to Ma the way Matthew's touch had felt brushing her cheek, and she tried to capture the words to describe his stare as he took her picture, how in that moment, she had never felt more beautiful.

And then she looked back at Ma, and expected to hear a scolding of her disapproval, but she just stared at her daughter with a look that was simply one thing. Love.

Ma put down the peeler. She wiped her hands on her apron and came and stood in the window next to her daughter. Laura continued. "Ma, I just was lost, you know." Ma nodded.

"It was like I couldn't tell my own body apart from Norman's body. And then the children had the whooping cough, and all night and all day, I was in a wash of sweat…theirs and mine. And Henry," Laura turned to her mother, "I couldn't count on him Ma. It was all me. All of the time. Until I didn't even know what was me, what was them, and if I was even a wife anymore, or his mother too," she sounded angrier and angrier recounting the feelings long stuffed away.

"And then," Ma said, "someone came along and made you feel beautiful." And Ma said it with a tone that meant she understood.

"But Ma," you always told me, "vanity is a sin." Laura turned slowly back to look out the window at her little girl with a huge piece of firewood in her arms, trudging back and forth from the woodshed to the front porch. "And now I know why you said that Ma. Because once I felt beautiful, I wanted to feel that way again and again and again. It was like an elixir that I couldn't get enough of."

"Laura," Ma said with a firm tone that was mostly reserved for Pa, "you know that is not why your Normy died. Tell me you know that girl. Get that right out of your fool head."

"But Ma, I lied. I cheated on Henry. I have kept this secret like a burning sore inside of me."

"Laura, don't be foolish. The Lord took Norman to ease his suffering, and that is the end of it."

Ma stood looking out the window. "He took Normy, and my Roger, and Ruth's Little Jannie." Her voice trailed off, "The Lord giveth…and the Lord taketh away."

Ma and Laura went back to the business of getting Thanksgiving dinner on the table. Aunt Hildy and Henry would be arriving any minute.

Chapter 60:

Laura could not eat another bite of Thanksgiving dinner when Ma appeared at the table with one of her famous pumpkin custard pies. She would have to have a slice of that! With the taste of sugar still on her lips, she felt the baby within her start to do flips and turns. She took Henry's hand and placed it on her tummy, "Another girl with a sweet tooth is on the way I believe," she said with a twinkle in her eye.

Henry had been right to send Laura to Walker Hill. The minute he arrived with his sister Hildy he could see that a sparkle was beginning to return to her eyes, and little Rose was rosy cheeked and bright eyed too. A dose of the simple goodness of life on the Walker Hill Farm, well, Henry knew from personal experience, it was sometimes all a person needed.

With tummies stuffed full to overflowing with Ma's delicious, hearty and simple Thanksgiving fare, Pa, Aunt Hildy and Henry retired to the sitting room in front of the warm wood fire. They chatted a bit, pulled out a checkerboard, but soon each was fast asleep. Little Rose played with her paper dolls on the floor. Laura and Ma worked side by side to tackle the dishes. Ma always took out her most delicate green and pink bone china wedding set, edged with tiny rosettes, for Thanksgiving, Christmas, and Easter dinners.

Once the final dish was wiped and placed carefully on the shelf, Ma invited Laura outside for a little after-dinner stroll. They both bundled up in their coats and scarves and took in the cold air sharply as they walked out the front door. "Laura," Ma said. " I want to talk about what happened downtown with that photographer all those years ago."

Laura nodded, secretly pleased that Ma hadn't shut the door on this conversation. Ma continued with purpose, "Laura. I know you are struggling, feeling guilty about that kiss or whatever the two of you were up to," Ma said quickly pushing past that particular uncomfortable part of the conversation. "Not that it matters what you were up to at this point," and then Ma stopped in her steps and looked directly into Laura's eyes.

"Laura," she said sternly, "There is no need to tell this story to Henry." And then she continued walking. "There I said it. That's what I wanted to say. Do not tell Henry," without a shred of hesitation Ma repeated this directive twice.

"But Ma," Laura started, but Ma quickly interrupted.

"Laura. There is no need. None at all. Listen to this old lady. Henry doesn't need to know. It'll do no good at all," and they kept walking down over the slope of the hill.

Laura had long thought that holding onto this secret was as big of a sin as actually kissing Matthew. Was Ma right that she needn't tell Henry what happened? This hadn't occurred to her before. Was it okay to hold onto a secret?

The two, mother and daughter walked in silence, arm and arm. When they turned around to walk back up Walker Hill, Ma paused when they were within earshot of the house. "Laura. You and Henry have both had enough heartbreak for a lifetime. Why break his heart again just to ease your guilt?"

Laura nodded. Ma went on, "Make your peace with your own self Laura. I was there and I saw you. You were overwhelmed. You were tired. You made a mistake. That's all that needs to be said. Forgive yourself and leave this in the past."

Laura's eyes burned with tears. Could Ma be right? Could she simply forgive herself and move on with the secret tucked away.

On the way into the house, Ma quietly whispered to her daughter, "Everyone dies with one little secret or another."

Ma's words were comforting, but Laura knew, although she didn't say so, she knew that wasn't true. Norman hadn't a single secret. Laura spent all of her time with him, and she felt he left this earth with her knowing all of his thoughts. But, in that moment, she knew she would die with this secret safely stowed away.

Chapter 61:

After Thanksgiving, Laura, Rose and Henry returned to their warm little parsonage in Mechanic Falls with a renewed outlook on the future. Henry snipped pine boughs from the backyard, and Laura wove them into a garland to hang over their front door. Rose and Laura sat by the fire in the evening and threaded popcorn and cranberries for their little blue spruce tree in the corner. The house was fragranced for the season...all cinnamon and evergreen.

Since their return from the farm on Walker Hill, Henry and Laura began to get excited about the baby that was on the way. Laura enthusiastically began to knit and sew tiny outfits, and she had Henry put the crib together.

Laura's daily rhythm had been so tied into Norman's needs and rituals, that she found it was very important to stick to a schedule to keep her mind and her hands busy. Any down time left her heart longing for the touch and sounds of her boy.

Laura, still not able to return to the front pew of the church, found comfort in the soothing and familiar sounds of her husband's sermons, and the music of the church, the words of the hymns filled her aching heart each Sunday.

With her boy in heaven, Laura listened with a renewed urgency and need, to the words of the scripture, to the lyrics in the hymnals.

Although she knew she could not compare her suffering to that of Job, she found great comfort held within Job's stories. After one sermon in which Henry referenced the scripture of Job time and again, Laura went home and wrote her favorite passages in her daily journaling.

JOB 12: 7 – 10: *"But ask the animals and they will teach you, or the birds in the sky, and they will tell you; or speak to the earth, and it will teach you, or let the fish in the sea inform you. Which of all these does not know that the hand of the LORD has done this? In his hand is the life of every creature and the breath of all mankind."*

She would read and reread these words, and imagine her life as a child on Walker Hill. She would think of birds popping in and out of the wild fields on the hill, and each peculiar and familiar call of the different bird species. The "caw " of the crows, the "cheeps" of the hummingbirds, the "trill" of the juncos, the distinct "chick-a-dee dee dee" of the black capped chickadee.

As Laura closed her eyes, and pictured each bird, imagining their colors, their calls, their tiny bodies, she found comfort. Knowing each tiny magnificent bird was the work of the Lord, made her smile and somehow feel more connected to her boy in heaven.

On another Sunday, Laura heard the words of Psalms 96: 11- 12: *"Let the heavens rejoice, let the earth be glad; let the sea resound, and all that is in it. Let the fields be jubilant, and everything in them; let all the trees of the forest sing with joy."*

Nearly bursting with child, Laura began throwing herself into nature. Anything that connected her to the earth made her feel closer to the boy who was now one with the earth.

She would read books about Northeastern bird species and then she would find the seeds and the nuts and the fruits that would bring the birds to her front porch. Laura knew their calls, and would stand on her front steps, hand outstretched, calling the birds to feed from her palm.

Henry marveled at his wife's knowledge about each and every bird in their trees in Mechanic Falls, and although he was not sure of her motivation, he knew that when she was feeding her birds she was happy, and that was all that mattered to him.

When at last Laura gave birth to their third child, a perfect little girl named Helen, immediately after mother and child were released from the hospital, Laura had her little baby bundled in a swaddle of blankets and outside. She parked the carriage right next to her, while she stretched out her hand full of sunflower seeds and fed her bold little chickadees.

The minute the snow disappeared from the borders surrounding the parsonage, Laura began to work the soil with a hoe, and loosen the dirt for the flower beds she had been planning all winter. Members of the congregation marveled in the summertime, remarking on the beauty of the parsonage which was surrounded by robust blooms and blossoms of all shapes and colors and glorious wafting scents.

Laura could nearly always be found outside, tending, pruning and coaxing her plants. She found enormous satisfaction in the process of taking a seed and watching it grow, but nothing made her feel more proud than when a dying plant could be brought back to life with her tender care.

Laura felt the same way about any of God's creatures. One day she and Helen came upon a tiny scarlet tanager, near their hedges, sitting there, helpless, with a broken wing. By the time Rose had gotten home from school, the little bird was in a cage with a makeshift splint on its wing and her mother, Laura, was tenderly feeding the brilliant red bird with an eyedropper. Eventually, the splint was removed from the black broken wing, and the entire family released it successfully into the oak trees in the back of the parsonage. Laura cried with elation when she watched it fly away, and the girls cheered for the victorious ending.

Whenever Laura was able to bring a plant or a bird or a bloom back from the brink of death, she silently asked why it was she was not able to do the same for her boy.

Chapter 62:

The girls grew to be strong and healthy and secure in the small circle comprising their lives: home, church and school.

Henry and Laura were disciplined about saving their money so they could buy a small piece of property of their own. Having always lived in a parsonage owned by the church was difficult, because at the end of the day, they always knew any changes they made were really not their own, so the day they bought their own tiny cabin in the Maine woods was a joyful day.

Rose took her little sister, Helen's, hand in hers and climbed the rickety little staircase to find a perfect little loft bedroom which they would claim as their own. Henry proudly went to the shed to inspect the hand pump, which provided fresh drinking water from an icy mountain spring, and he diligently checked on the woodstove, their only source of heat.

As the family explored the inside of the cottage, Laura dropped to her knees in the front yard, and pulled the mossy earth from its roots and raised the soil to her nose, taking in the strong woodsy scent of the soil. This smell was a blessing...the smell of all of the rich possibilities that would happen in this ground. She knew she would be able to create small daily miracles by using this soil, and this was all she could or would ask for. She had a plot of land to call her own.

Laura could hear the sounds of her family inside of the cottage, rattling and running to and fro. She closed her eyes and listened. She could hear the laughter of her girls, the soothing voice of her husband, the distant croaks of bullfrogs in the nearby creek, and the steady trill of sparrows in the branches overhead.

Laura felt the welcome return of a simple emotion she had long forgotten. Gratitude.

Chapter 63:

Anne Morrow Lindbergh became one of Laura's heroines later in life. Her words spoke to Laura like no other, most likely because she, too, knew the sorrow of losing a child.

One evening Laura copied these words into her journal:

It isn't for the moment you are struck that you need courage, but for the long uphill climb back to sanity, and faith and security.

She simply entered one line of her own: Truer words were never spoken.

Laura had placed, all by hand, assorted red bricks pushed into the soil of her front yard, forming a lovely makeshift patio. In and about the bricks, she placed terra cotta plant pots filled with all of her favorite herbs: lavender, thyme, sage, peppermint, cilantro, rosemary, oregano, and spearmint. The pots were full and fragrant and well tended.

Around the border of her brick patio she planted her perennial garden that somehow seemed to thrive in spite of the acidic soil scattered with pine needles. Her patio was lined and trimmed in lambs ear, and golden glow, hosta and beach roses. She had fashioned a trellis for her clematis and the purple blossoms bravely clung to the branches.

Laura had just filled up her watering can from the hand pump when a car pulled up in front of the cottage. She ran to greet her long lost friend. It had been too many years.

Flora slowly got out from behind the steering wheel and seemed to be dwarfed by the size of her car. She was clearly cranky and annoyed by having to grab her cane from the back seat, but then smiled brilliantly when she spotted Laura running toward her. "Well aren't you just the prettiest sight for these old sore eyes," Flora yelled to her dear old friend.

Laura looped her arm in and around Flora's to help her gain her balance as she walked up the stone steps to Laura and Henry's cottage. Flora visibly caught her breath when she saw the beautiful garden in front of her. She turned warmly to Laura, and said, "Well, I would ask what you've been up to, but it's pretty plain to see exactly what's kept you busy." Laura beamed with pride as Flora limped her way across and through Laura's glorious masterpiece.

Laura produced a tray with hot tea and ginger snaps, and served it to Flora in the center of her garden. Flora looked long and hard at Laura, and placed her wrinkled hand on top of Laura's garden worn fingers. "And how have you been my dear friend?" There was no need for small talk between these two women.

Laura sighed, and picked up her teacup. "I miss my son, Flora," she said unabashedly. "I miss Normy every, single day." Flora nodded.

"You know Flora, people say strange things when you lose a boy like Norman," and Laura's voice cracked.

"They say things like: it was a blessing, and they indicate that it must somehow be a relief."

Flora nodded, and said finally, "They don't understand, Laura."

Laura agreed, "No, they don't," and she paused before continuing. "Raising a boy like Norman is different because you actually, if it is possible, grow closer to this child than children who are more typical. In order to survive their upbringing, you almost have to be one in the same with them."

Laura continued, "Because he couldn't talk, I talked for him. Because he couldn't walk, I was his legs. Because he couldn't tend to himself, I had to anticipate all of his needs," and it was then that tears escaped Laura's eyes, "and when he was gone, that part of me that I had developed out of necessity...well, I had no idea what to do with that part...it was like a useless limb."

Flora jumped in at that, "And so Laura, you have had to get to know yourself all over again."

Laura nodded. "I have, and truthfully, I didn't even know where to begin," and then she added, " so I had to go all of the way back to where I came from."

Flora knew just what Laura meant. "Walker Hill?"

"Yes," Laura said with glistening eyes, "Walker Hill."

Chapter 64:

Just like a broken limb needs time and immobility to heal. So, too, does the heart.

In the quiet of the forest grove, in the tiny cabin owned by Reverend and Mrs. Brooks, the nights were spent in ways, at the time, which seemed unremarkable, and yet, upon reflection, they were quite remarkable.

Reverend Brooks spent his time reading and finding inspiration in the pages of the Bible and preparing for his upcoming sermons. Rose, a talented student, would spend her evenings, without reminders, studying for her high school courses. Little Helen often worked on her paint by numbers or her puzzles, and she would ask her sister and her mother to teach her to crochet.

Laura would finish tidying her little kitchen until it was spotless, hanging each cup and positioning each saucer, and then she would sit down to write in her journal. Inspired by Anne Morrow Lindbergh, she would write down a quote and then often would write her reflection about that quote. She found that gardening during the daytime, writing when surrounded by her family at night, she was beginning to feel like herself again.

But she knew, it was not possible to rush the healing of the heart.

She copied these words from Lindbergh:

The sea does not reward those who are too anxious, too greedy, or too impatient. To dig for treasures shows not only impatience and greed, but lack of faith. Patience, patience, patience is what the sea teaches. Patience and faith. One should lie empty, open, choiceless as a beach – waiting for a gift from the sea.

And then Laura wrote her simple response*: Today I laid the face of a sunflower on a stump, sunny-side up. I sat as still as a stone next to that stump and I waited for a forest friend to appear. It only took about five minutes until a brave chipmunk appeared. He seemed to look me over, and size me up. He decided to trust me, and he filled his cheeks several times with the plump seeds. My patience was rewarded by making a new, special friend from the forest glen.*

Chapter 65:

The simple rituals of life and the treasures found in nature were the balm that healed Laura's broken heart.

As the years passed bringing forward all of Maine's glorious and ever changing seasons, so too did Laura's lustrous chestnut hair turn snowy white, and Henry's full head of hair transformed to a single ring of sparse hair around a growing, shiny bald spot.

The cottage in the grove became one with its owners. The treads up the narrow staircase wore the artistic renderings of Henry's imagination, and the wainscoting on the walls were painted with bright and primitive scenery, all taken from the coast of Maine or from the farmlands of Walker Hill.

There was hardly a surface that didn't hold the artwork of the proprietors. Laura had become a wonderful quilter, and any scraps of fabrics were quickly turned into pieces of intricately hand sewn quilts.

Rose and Helen had become mothers themselves, and each grandchild, upon arrival, was greeted with a quilt that would capture the attention and admiration of all who saw it, newly presented, and gratefully accepted, at the hospital.

Any guest who arrived at the home of Reverend Brooks was greeted with the fragrance of freshly herbed stews boiling on the cookstove, and Laura was never too busy to present the guests with a steeping pot of tea, "no different than was served to Queen Elizabeth, except the pot that held it," Laura usually quipped to quote her beloved late mother from Walker Hill.

When the grandchildren visited the "grove," their toys were always handmade. Henry would carve wooden cars and train cars for the children to play with, and he also presented each granddaughter with a wooden Mouse House. The grandchildren delighted in spending hours, carpeting the floors, using empty spools of thread for the furniture, and they would frame tiny postage stamps as art work for the walls.

Laura sewed tiny mice for the house, complete with dresses and aprons for the females and overalls for the boys.

The grandchildren would arrive for a week at a time, and Henry and Laura would teach them to sit very still, with an outstretched hand filled with seeds, and if they were very patient and still...a black capped chickadee would come along and land on their small eager fingertips to pluck up the sunflower seeds.

Laura's gardens became magic fairylands for the children. It was there that they pretended to be kings and queens of the land, and it was there that they learned the difference between a daisy and a brown-eyed Susan, and a lily of the valley from a forget me not.

It was also in that hallowed garden that each subsequent generation learned that you cannot separate the lessons learned in nature from the lessons learned in life.

In the fall, the last of the blooms would wither and fade and eventually die, but Laura would explain to her grandchildren, as she caressed the dying blooms, "But there is always hope, even in death, because these beautiful blooms will leave behind their seeds, and in the spring, when it is still impossibly cold, a new green sprout will shoot up from the frozen earth, and a new flower will come adorn our garden plot in the spring."

Laura had painted a large flat stone in her garden, and it said: *Women need solitude in order to find the true essence of themselves.*

Chapter 66:

It was an unremarkable night when Henry clutched his chest and died on the floor of the cottage. He never spoke a single word before he was gone.

As Laura recounted this event to her daughters, she was still in shock. Their father had gotten up to use the bathroom in the deep of night. She thought maybe he had heartburn as often was the case. He stepped down the narrow, creaky staircase, quietly so as not to wake her, and then she heard a horrible crash as he neared the bottom of the staircase. She never even remembered jumping out of bed, but remembered being at his side.

And he was gone. She called an ambulance, but they could do nothing to revive him.

There went the only person on earth who shared her journey, and who shared her sorrow. Not only did she lose her husband, she lost her last remaining connection to the life before it all...the life with Norman.

At Henry's graveside, Laura quietly thanked her mother for the advice she had given decades before. His heart had already been broken by the loss of his son. She decided in that moment, the most loving thing she did, was hold this secret inside of herself to avoid breaking a good man's heart for a second time.

Epilogue:

Almost a decade after I sat in my living room, sipping wine, and learning the story of my grandmother, Laura, I got a divorce anyway.

I was terrified to tell Grammy, as she had made it clear to me that happiness should never be my goal. For years her story hung in the air for me. So I would journey on. Discontent, edgy, frustrated, unfulfilled.

Eventually, after I was living apart from my soon-to-be-ex-husband, I mustered up the courage to invite Grammy to lunch to tell her about my personal failure and my imminent divorce. I picked her up in a looming antiquated brick building, next to the public library. This building had recently become her home. When walking on icy pathways to fill her wood box for the wood heat in wintertime became too much for her, she moved into this third story apartment, away from her cottage in the woods. A pretty gutsy move, for a pretty gutsy lady. She was 87 years old when she moved.

I brought her to my favorite funky little restaurant two blocks from her apartment. I was nervous as we sat down in a relatively private corner table. Grammy lifted her menu and began to study the options. I lifted mine, pretending I had any sort of an appetite. The thought of disappointing my grandmother had my stomach in knots.

"Grammy," I stammered, and she quickly interrupted my thought as she asked me if I had ever tried the ratatouille before. I never had.

"Oh, I don't know if I would like it, but it sure is fun to say," she remarked, and then she repeated the word a few more times, "Ratatouille, ratatouille, ratatouille. I'm practicing for when I order." And then, with a devilish wink, she asked, "Will we be having wine?"

"Grammy, of course," I affirmed immediately, "always wine," and she nodded in full agreement. When Grammy lived in the grove, I would notice her pouring herself a tiny thimbleful of sherry every now and again, but this "city living," and perhaps living into her 80's, had given her a new appreciation for spirits.

"Always wine," she repeated. "And let's not forget," she added decisively, "always dessert at my age too."

God, I loved this woman.

"Grammy," I blurted out, "I am getting a divorce." I waited, and she put down her menu and fixed her stare on me, over the top of her glasses. I tried to read her expression.

There was a pause. I expected there would be.

"Oh," she finally said, seemingly nonplussed, "I'm not surprised."

And that was that. No judgment. No tone. Just: "I'm not surprised."

So I couldn't let it go at that. It was too easy. "Grammy," I said, "what about what you said to me, all of those years ago?"

"What did I say?" she responded curiously.

"You said there was nowhere in the Bible that said that I needed to be happy," I reminded her.

"Well," she continued, "there *isn't* anywhere in the Bible that says you need to be happy. That was true."

"But Grammy, when you said that, I thought you meant I should never get a divorce," I felt the whole universal belief system upon which I had made enormous decisions crumbling beneath my feet.

Gram took a sip of her pinot grigio, seeming to really enjoy bringing the goblet to her lips, "I didn't say that did I?"

"Well, you implied it," I shot right back.

"I simply told you there is no place in the Bible that prioritizes your happiness," and she put down her wine, and leaned forward. "Who knows? Maybe if I would have had a good job like yours, I would have gotten a divorce too?"

Wait. What?

"But what about the life you shared? Walker Hill? The gardens," and then I threw in, "Norman?"

Gram never blinked. "Well, your grandfather could be a real poop sometimes you know. He was not an easy man."

I was flabbergasted. Gram seemed to enjoy my discomfort with this whole thing.

"Hey, I didn't have any money. It wasn't like today. I mean, I loved your grandfather, don't get me wrong," and again, she leaned in for the kill, "but different times, different circumstances, well, I may have ditched him too."

I could not hide my disbelief with what she was saying. "Gram," I started...

"Oh don't get all excited about what I'm saying. I didn't divorce him. I stayed with him. Our life was good at times, bad at times. It was just that. Our life. Your life is your life. We all do what we have to do with what's in front of us," and she dipped her fork back into her ratatouille.

"You know," Gram added, "Everyone has a story that can make you cry."

After a few moments, Gram put down her fork. "It's good," she said dabbing her mouth in the corners with her napkin. "I guess I like ratatouille, but I'm going to be sure to save room for dessert."

In the midst of winter, I found there was within me, an invincible summer. And that makes me happy. For it says that no matter how hard the world pushes against me, within me, there's something stronger – something better, pushing right back. –Albert Camus

Acknowledgements:

I would like to thank my husband for tolerating (and possibly enjoying) the hours and hours of silence, as I type away the afternoons and evenings, lost in thought and away on Walker Hill.

I am so grateful to my wonderful friends and colleagues who allow me to share my history, listen to my stories and my thinking, and encourage me to continue to write.

Thank you to my mother, Diana Berry, and my father, Tom Rowe, and my sister, Kathy LeMieux...for editing, proofreading, and for always cheering me forward to the finish line.

A special shout out and thank you to my colleague and friend, Sam Dunbar. Sam did all of the tedious and meticulous editing. He managed to get the job done, and make me laugh all the way through with his hilarious quips in the margins.

Thank you to my children. They continually inspire me to be the best version of myself.

Finally, I thank my maternal and paternal grandmothers, Harriet Rowe Niles and Ilse Rowe Jonson. Both women were fiercely strong, each in her own way. They both endured great personal hardship and persevered through it all...teaching the generations that followed, although no one gets out of this life unscathed, there is great beauty to be found in every lesson learned.

Made in the USA
Middletown, DE
26 September 2019